Praise for Moira Rogers's
Haunted Sanctuary

"If you're interested in hot shifters, scarred pasts and a whole lotta steam, check out this new series."
~ *USA TODAY*

"This story starts out with a bang and the action rarely lets up until the very exciting climax of the story."
~ *Coffee Time Romance*

"Filled with dynamic action, heartbreaking drama, and enough hot, intense loving that will have you wanting your very own alpha wolf; this supernatural thriller is guaranteed to keep you hooked till the very end."
~ *Smexy Books*

"At a time when wolves aren't necessarily a new thing in Paranormal Romance, Moira Rogers somehow brings forth a fresh approach, making me fall in love with the werewolf all over again."
~ *Under the Covers Book Blog*

"*Haunted Sanctuary* hits the ground running fast and furiously, pounding the reader with action and emotion immediately."
~ *Joyfully Reviewed*

Look for these titles by
Moira Rogers

Now Available:

Southern Arcana
Crux
Crossroads
Deadlock
Cipher
Impulse
Enigma

Red Rock Pass
Cry Sanctuary
Sanctuary Lost
Sanctuary's Price
Sanctuary Unbound

Building Sanctuary
A Safe Harbor
Undertow

Bloodhounds
Wilder's Mate
Hunter's Prey
Archer's Lady
Diana's Hound

...and the Beast
Sabine
Kisri

Children of the Undying
Demon Bait
Hammer Down

Green Pines Sanctuary
Haunted Sanctuary
Haunted Wolves

Print Collections
Sanctuary
Sanctuary Redeemed
Building Sanctuary
Shadowed Moon
Shattered Moon

Haunted Sanctuary

Moira Rogers

SAMHAIN
PUBLISHING

Samhain Publishing, Ltd.
11821 Mason Montgomery Road, 4B
Cincinnati, OH 45249
www.samhainpublishing.com

Haunted Sanctuary
Copyright © 2014 by Moira Rogers
Print ISBN: 978-1-61921-637-2
Digital ISBN: 978-1-61921-220-6

Editing by Anne Scott
Cover by Angela Waters

First Samhain Publishing, Ltd. electronic publication: January 2013
First Samhain Publishing, Ltd. print publication: January 2014

Dedication

This is for our editor, Anne Scott. Four years ago, she bought a book called *Cry Sanctuary*, and we've never looked back. Thank you for believing in us, even when we make that almost impossible to do, and for continuing to support us, even when we go a little nuts.

Chapter One

Practically the whole damn town was asleep already.

Here and there, tiny pockets of activity caught Jay Ancheta's eye as he maneuvered his SUV through the darkened streets. A handful of high school kids drifted out of the athletics building behind the football field, undoubtedly players leaving a late practice. A few storefronts still glowed with faint light, owners sticking around to handle inventory or bookkeeping, and he made a mental note to check again on his way back into town.

For now, he had a destination in mind, and he could only wish the adrenaline pumping through his veins had more to do with the job at hand...and less to do with seeing Eden Green.

He pulled into the parking lot on the east side of the library. The windows upstairs were dark, but before he could wonder where Eden might be, he spotted her coming out the back exit. She wore no sweater or jacket, only slacks and a lightweight white shirt, though the breeze tossed her blonde hair as she paused to lock the door.

As soon as Jay stepped out of his vehicle, he caught the sweet citrus scent of her shampoo. "Eden."

She whirled with a sharp, in-drawn breath, but the tension in her face vanished when she squinted through the darkness and caught sight of him. "Jay, thank God. You startled me."

"Sorry about that." He leaned against the front fender of his SUV, adopting the least threatening pose he could manage. "I was hoping to catch you before you locked up for the night."

Blushing, she turned back to the door and turned the key with a click. "If no one's here, sometimes I lock up a little early. There's a television show I like to watch..." Her voice trailed off as she reached the parking lot, her gaze taking in his uniform. "Is this official business? Nothing's happened, has it? My father—"

"Hale and hardy when I saw him this afternoon," Jay cut in. "It's nothing like that. I had a question, that's all, about Green Pines."

"About the farm?" She stopped a few paces shy of him and tilted her head. "What do you need to know?"

Her heart was beating fast, and Jay drew in another breath, grateful for the shift in the wind that carried her scent away this time. "I'd have asked your dad when I was at the diner today, but you're listed as the property owner of record. The Wilsons called me, said they heard car engines and commotion out there a couple nights ago. Do you know anything about that?"

"A commotion?" She frowned. "No, there shouldn't be anyone out there. Unless the teenagers you ran off last summer decided it was safe again..."

"No, I doubt that." *Damn it.* "Just to be safe, I'll ride out tonight and take a look around."

She lifted her keys. "I'll follow you."

Eden Green might look every inch the bashful small-town librarian, but she'd reportedly inherited her mother's legendary stubborn streak, and forbidding her from joining him would only get her back up. "I'd rather you didn't. An abandoned farm's mighty attractive to someone looking for a place to conduct all kinds of illegal business. It could be dangerous."

For a moment she considered him, her teeth working at her lower lip. "I'd like to come," she said finally. "I can ride with you, if you prefer, and stay in the SUV until you're sure there aren't any criminals."

Her blue eyes were clouded, but with something more complex than mere curiosity or even outrage that someone might be trespassing on her property. She had reasons for asking, reasons that left anxiety and a strange sort of expectation hanging in the air, and Jay found himself nodding. "It's your place. Ride with me and I'll make sure you stay safe."

"I know you will." She smiled and tucked her keys into her purse. "Thank you, Jay. It means a lot to know you're keeping an eye on things. I keep hoping my father will let me at least *try* to sell the farm, but...well. Family is complicated."

"So I hear." Family, he knew little about. Pack, on the other hand, could be both simple and tragically convoluted. "And looking out for you is my job. Now hop in."

Eden circled the car and slid onto the passenger seat, fiddling with the belt long after she'd buckled it. Her fingers slid up and down the nylon in near-silent strokes he could hear as clearly as her still-racing heart.

She was hiding something.

Jay cranked the engine and pulled onto the main road before speaking. "Anything you want to tell me, Eden?"

She started and shook her head with a shaky laugh. "I'm nervous, that's all. When I was a kid, I thought the farm was haunted, you know."

"Uh-huh." The place looked it, spooky and practically abandoned, but it also wasn't the true motivation for her galloping pulse. "Try again?"

She sighed softly. "Do you listen to town gossip? The older stories?"

"On occasion."

"Green Pines Farm has provided its share over the years."

They could talk in circles all the way out of town, but it would get them nowhere. "Sweetheart, why don't you just tell me who you expect us to find out there?"

"I don't *expect* anyone," she protested. "But my father always hopes that my cousin will come back. That's why he doesn't want me to sell the farm. He wants Zack's inheritance intact."

Zack Green, not quite the prodigal son. Town gossip held that his father, Eden's uncle, had run him out of town at eighteen—all because he suspected another man had really fathered the boy. "How much of it is true? The talk about Zack's mother?"

"All of it, and then some." Eden's voice held a sharp edge, but as she continued, it mellowed into sadness. "My uncle wasn't Zack's father, and everyone in the family knew it. But he took it out on Zack more often than not, and my father didn't care for that."

Jay slowed for a red light and turned his upper body to face Eden's. "Good. Circumstances of birth aren't exactly within a kid's control."

Eden glanced at him, her features only clear in the darkness because of his sharpened vision. She probably thought he couldn't see the way she opened her mouth and closed it several times before wetting her lips nervously. "Uncle Albus—" Her fingers tightened into fists. "He was an angry man. Once his wife ran off, the only kindness Zack ever saw was from my parents."

And she felt guilty about that, though she'd been no more to blame for Zack's situation than he himself had. "Eden, if your cousin *is* out at the farm, we'll help him. Whatever he needs."

"It's probably not him. I don't think he'd come back here unless he had no other choice. But thank you."

They'd reached the edge of town already, and Jay took the right-hand turn that led toward the farm. "Don't mention it."

She hadn't told him everything. He could hear it in the slightly high-pitched tone of her voice, see it in her unwillingness to meet his eyes. Little Eden Green was still hiding something, but Jay had no high ground there.

After all, he'd never told her he was a werewolf.

Next to him, Eden fidgeted. "If it *is* him..."

"What is it? Drugs?"

"No! No, not drugs. Not Zack." She hesitated, and he knew from her pounding heart and shallow breath that she was getting ready to lie to him again. "I think he's involved with people who are into them, though. Dangerous people."

Soft moonlight drifted through the canopy of trees bending over the disused drive. "People you think might have come here with him?"

"Maybe."

God damn it. "Then I shouldn't have brought you along."

"I'm probably overreacting," she said quickly, as if concerned he'd turn the car around. "It's probably those teenagers, breaking into the old barn to party again."

She might be jumping to conclusions, but her fear was real. It prickled over his skin and raised the hairs on the back of his neck, and his unease deepened as he pulled up the long, gravel drive.

Everything looked dark from a distance, but not completely. At second glance, Jay could see the farmhouse's windows glowing with faint flickers of light, as if candles or kerosene lamps were burning beyond the tattered curtains.

It wasn't until they were a third of the way up the driveway that the moon illuminated the vehicles parked at haphazard angles across the front lawn of the main house—two trucks and a shiny silver sedan. Jay stared at the trucks as he parked his own SUV and cut the engine. "Shelby County plates," he murmured. "Has your cousin been in Memphis?"

"I don't know." That, at least, sounded like the truth. "I think he called my father from there once."

"Do you think his friends are—" A slice of sound caught his attention, and he jerked at his seatbelt as he tried to pinpoint its source.

Snarls. Whines. The snap of jaws and teeth.

"Stay here," he told Eden. Too clipped, brusque, but he needed for her to understand. "Get down and stay here, no matter what happens. Say it."

Her eyes blazed with irritation, as if she wasn't used to orders, but she wasn't stupid, either. She unfastened her belt and hunched low in the seat. "I'll stay here."

Did she know? Her warnings had been vague but desperate, as if she suspected the truth and wanted to tell him but didn't know how. "If things go south, get your ass over here behind the wheel and get back to town." But Jay trembled, his hand on the door. He couldn't leave her alone and unarmed, so he unsnapped his holster and held out his pistol. "If you *have* to, if anything comes after you—"

Her fingers brushed his, but she didn't take the gun. "You hear something."

She knew, all right. "Anything, Eden. Point and shoot, then get the hell out of here."

His need to protect her still at odds with his duty, Jay took off around the side of the house. The sounds of fighting grew louder as he approached the woods behind the barn, and he stopped and stripped off his clothes as quickly as possible.

As soon as he knelt and coaxed the slow burn of magic inside him into the conflagration that would bring his change, Jay caught sight of a man dragging a woman out of the trees.

14

Her pink hair stood out in the moonlight, a bright spot of color against the dark forest.

Her attacker jerked to a halt, his head whipping toward Jay. His mouth curved into a feral smile, undoubtedly at catching Jay in the vulnerable moments just before a shift. But as the stranger took a step forward, the girl twisted, raking her nails across his cheek in a desperate attempt to escape.

He slapped her hard enough to drive her to her knees, and Jay took advantage of the man's distraction to finish his transformation. Wild, instinctive satisfaction filled him. If the stranger thought him weak, that it would take him long minutes to struggle through the change from man to wolf, he'd be fatally disappointed.

Jay sprang forward with a growl.

The man spun, wrenching his body out of the path of Jay's charge with an angry roar. The girl scrambled to her feet with the speed of a werewolf and bolted.

"Mae!" The shouted name rode an angry command, sizzling dominant power that ghosted past Jay and slammed into the girl's back like a physical blow. She hit the ground on her knees, shaking. "Don't run, darling. You and I are going to have a talk about all this disobedience." The man whipped a knife out of his boot as he turned on Jay. "Just as soon as I teach this packless mutt a lesson."

The knife looked normal, but it felt like magic. Jay circled, his teeth bared in a snarl as the man watched him, no hint of fear in his cruel eyes. When he moved, it was blindingly fast, the blade slashing toward Jay's side.

The wicked edge found its mark, slicing a burning but shallow line across Jay's ribs. Definitely magic, because a heaviness accompanied the pain, a stagnant weight instead of the delicate tickle of near-instantaneous healing. Jay twisted and snapped at the man's arm, grazing skin with teeth just as sharp as the knife.

15

His opponent jerked back with a laugh. "Yeah, you feel it, don't you? You can bite me and I'll heal. You'll just keep bleed—" Twigs snapped to their left, and the man lunged fast enough to get a handful of the girl's pink hair and jerk her off her feet as she tried to run. "You treacherous *bitch!*"

The lunge stretched out the line of his body, leaving him low and open to attack. Jay dug his back legs into the soft earth and launched himself at the man's throat. He closed his teeth on the vulnerable spot and felt flesh give and blood run hot as his momentum carried them both to the ground.

Another wolf snarled at the edge of the trees. Beneath Jay, his enemy struggled weakly. The girl kicked the knife away from his outstretched hand and grabbed it as she rolled to her feet. She held the blade awkwardly, as if she didn't know how to use it, and backed away, brandishing the weapon at the new wolf.

The wolf ignored her and charged at Jay. The girl shouted one word, her voice high and panicked. "Zack!"

Jay took the full weight of the charging wolf in the shoulder and rolled. He snapped viciously at the wolf's back legs and pushed up on his paws just in time to see three more wolves break out of the woods, a tall, bloodied man at their heels.

One of the new wolves dove toward Jay. A second lunged at the disheveled man, who caught the animal by the scruff of its neck and threw it toward the tree line with a roar of fury.

The creature hit a tree with a crack and fell to the ground, limp and twitching, but the man didn't stop or even slow down. He reached for another, and the fight turned quick and ugly as the remaining wolves attacked low, over and over, desperate to gain an advantage.

Teeth tore at flesh. Claws raked through clothes and skin alike. The man seemed as oblivious to the pain as he was to the pink-haired girl's broken noises of protest. He snapped necks and tore wolves apart, and when no more surged to take the place of the fallen, he whirled on Jay.

16

"Zack, no—" The girl stumbled forward. "He saved me. He killed Scott."

The change was hard, sometimes impossible, when a fight had Jay riding high on adrenaline. He called it anyway, and the effort hit him like a sprint, left him clutching a stitch in one side and the fiery cut on the other. "Zack?" he panted in disbelief. "Zack Green?"

The man's chest heaved. He wiped blood from his mouth before spitting on the ground. "Did you take care of the rest of them?"

Jay grabbed his pants and glanced around at the bodies scattered on the grass. "There are more?" As soon as his brain processed the thought, a cold chill gripped him. "Fuck."

Eden.

Eden watched the spot by the house where Jay had disappeared and cursed her cowardice.

She should have told him. There'd been a moment when she'd wondered if he knew already, and she should have seized it. Spilled out the truth—the messy, unbelievable truth—even if it meant he'd never look at her the same way again.

All her starry-eyed daydreams of him would mean nothing if a werewolf tore out his throat.

Stupid. Stupid, stupid, *stupid.*

The painful silence stretched out until Eden couldn't handle it anymore. Had Jay heard something? If so, it had been too quiet for her to pick up, but what else could have driven him from the car? She'd read stories of cops having hunches, gut instincts that seemed to border on psychic ability, but almost all seemed based on subconscious recognition of clues and the voice of experience.

Maybe Jay had experience with werewolves.

Maybe he was one.

She choked on a hysterical laugh and sank lower in the seat. It should have been ridiculous to imagine the Chief of Police as a big bad wolf, but the more she thought about it, the less she wanted to laugh.

Grace. Strength. Power. Her cousin had shared all of those traits, along with Jay's knack for knowing when trouble was near. But if Jay was a wolf, he was better at hiding his darker side than Zack had been. Everyone in town had recognized the feral edge under her cousin's anger. They'd treated him like a dangerous animal, one that might maul them at any second.

And, to be fair, he could have.

"Jay Ancheta might be a werewolf," she muttered out loud, forcing herself to acknowledge the absurdity of her own thoughts by giving them voice. Cringe-inducing, maybe...but with the night heavy and still around her, it didn't feel absurd.

She eased her hand away from the gun and reached into her purse in search of her phone. Her fingers had just brushed the edge of the case when a low snarl broke the silence.

"Shit." She dropped her purse and snatched up the gun, her pulse pounding. A man with dark hair slammed against the driver's side window, and she couldn't hold back her shriek of fear. Another clawed its way free of her throat as the man tugged at the door handle.

Locked. She'd remembered to lock them when Jay left, and her relief lasted all of five seconds before the man tore the door from its hinges in a screech of protesting metal.

Werewolves. It had to be. The only part of her mind not shaking in terror knew that nothing else explained the strength it would take to rip pieces from the vehicle.

It was that cool, calm part of her mind that pulled the trigger.

She'd braced herself as well as she could, but she still wasn't prepared for the recoil. Her hands jerked, sending her second shot through the windshield, and the wolf lunged into the car and ripped the gun from her hands before she could hiss out a pained breath. By the time she realized what had happened, his hands had closed around her upper arms.

Her shoulder crashed into the steering wheel as he dragged her across the seat. Fighting his grip was futile; he pulled her into the open and hoisted her up so she was face to face with his glowing yellow eyes.

Those eyes narrowed as he buried his nose in her neck and inhaled. "You don't smell like his bitch," the man muttered. "You're just a lousy fucking human."

The words didn't make sense. Had he expected her to smell like her cousin? Or could he smell another wolf in the SUV? *Jay*—

Jay should have come back by now.

She pushed the useless thought away and rammed her knee into her attacker's balls. He howled his pain, his rage, and threw her to the ground like a broken toy. His clothes ripped as he shifted, and he hit the ground on all fours, his hands and feet already turning to paws. Eden found herself staring into an open, snarling muzzle full of razor-sharp teeth.

She scrambled back, kicking at his nose when he lunged. His teeth closed on the heel of her boot, and she twisted and tried to jerk away, wrenching her ankle in the process.

Tears sprung to her eyes, but she bit her lip and pulled again, dragging her foot free of her shoe. Hope surged as she twisted again and landed on her hands and knees. If she could get under the car or to the house—

A growl ripped through the air a second before a heavy weight crashed into her, driving her to the ground. Claws dug into her body, but the pain disappeared under a flood of agony as the wolf sank sharp teeth into her arm.

Screaming. Running. A woman, a brunette dressed in flannel, yelling as she kicked at the wolf. "No!"

The wolf reared back, and the woman swung the butt end of a shotgun so hard it sounded like a solid home run when it connected with the animal's head. He tumbled off Eden and rolled away just far enough for the woman to ready the shotgun as he rose.

She fired once and the wolf staggered back with a howling whine. She worked the slide, fired again, and the wolf fell.

Eden struggled to her knees, her back on fire and her arm throbbing. "Where's Jay? The man I came with—"

The woman tore off her flannel shirt and wrapped it around Eden's wound. "We have to find Zack."

"Zack's here?" It was a stupid question, but it was hard to think when every heartbeat made the pain worse. "You're with him?"

"You're Eden." It wasn't a question. The brunette pulled her to her feet. "Can you walk?"

"I don't know." She took one tentative step and hissed as her ankle buckled. She pitched against the side of the SUV with a groan. "I need to find Jay. I didn't warn him, and I should have. I need to warn him."

"Shh." The woman tilted her head, then wrapped Eden's arm around her shoulders. "Come on, this way."

The world went gray with every step. Eden couldn't feel her fingers anymore, couldn't feel much of her hand at all on her bitten arm.

A bite. "Oh crap, the wolf bit me. Is that bad?"

Before the woman could answer, Jay ran out of the trees, barefoot with his shirt hanging open. "Jesus Christ. Eden?"

She stared at his chest. Beautiful light-brown skin and dark hair, muscles and strength, and if he'd been undressed, unarmed, he couldn't be human. "You're a wolf."

20

"You're bleeding." His gaze dropped to her arm, and he stepped forward to hold her up.

He hadn't denied it. He hadn't even *blinked*. "You're a wolf," she said again, more quietly this time. "I got bitten. Does that mean anything?"

He blanched. "Eden—"

The brunette cried out, a wordless noise of relief and worry tangled together. She jerked away and ran toward the trees, where Zack had walked out of the shadows, and threw her arms around his neck.

That it was Zack, Eden had no doubt. The eighteen-year-old hero she remembered was there, buried under blood and stress and numerous tattoos that circled his arms, crept up his shoulders and across his chest. He looked as if he'd only aged ten of the last twenty-two years, but pain had carved its mark in his eyes.

They held little recognition as they studied her, but that made sense. She'd been only ten years old the day he'd finally fled his father's temper.

She wet her dry lips. "Hi, Zack."

"Eden. Are you all right?" His gaze snapped to Jay, and something dangerous stirred in his eyes.

She didn't know how to answer.

"She's been bitten," Jay said evenly. "I need to take her to the hospital."

Finally, a normal suggestion. She clung to it with both hands, fighting back the feeling that the ground had turned to shifting sand beneath her. "Soon? I'm not doing so well."

"Scott's friend got to her," the brunette blurted in a desperate rush. "I know you told us to stay inside, but I had to stop him, Zack. I had to try."

Zack smoothed his hands over the girl's hair without taking his eyes off Jay and Eden. "Take her. We'll deal with the bodies."

Jay peeled back the edge of the makeshift flannel bandage and grimaced. "Let's go, honey. You'll do fine 'til we get there, but you'll need stitches." He lifted Eden off her feet and carried her to the battered SUV.

Holding back pained whimpers kept her distracted while he settled her on the front seat and buckled her in. By the time she'd gotten her breath, Jay was pulling down the driveway.

"You don't have a door," she protested belatedly.

He glanced at her, his jaw tight. "What are they going to do, arrest me?"

She couldn't help it. Whether it was pain or shock or the series of emotional blows she couldn't say, but it was too much. A hysterical, gasping laugh rasped out of her. "God, none of them would dare."

"I hope not." He pulled onto the main road and reached over to pat her leg. "You're going to be fine, Eden. The bleeding isn't severe. They'll be able to fix you right up."

Eden caught his hand and clung to it, scared that her good fingers had started to tingle. "Even though I was attacked by something they think doesn't exist?"

He hesitated. "As far as anyone at the ER will be able to tell, a dog bit you, okay?"

Still avoiding. She squeezed his hand. "Are you a werewolf, Jay?"

"I am." He slowed for a turn toward the highway. "So's your cousin, I guess. And the dangerous people after him?"

Swallowing hard, Eden closed her eyes. "I'm sorry. I didn't know how to tell you. I don't—I don't know much about werewolves, or what Zack's tangled up in. He tries to keep me and Dad out of it."

"I get it. You told me as much as you could without sounding crazy."

The tingling spread to her entire hand. If it hadn't been so intense, she might have suspected it was nothing more than her body's pleasure in touching Jay. Handsome, intelligent, wonderful Jay.

The werewolf.

"You didn't answer me," she said, trying to keep her voice calm. "Neither did the girl. I got bitten by a werewolf. Am I—" No, those words weren't going to come out sounding serene, no matter what she did.

He drew to a stop at a red light and sighed. "Eden, I don't know. It's not that simple. I've seen people with bites turn out to be completely unaffected. It doesn't mean you're going to turn into a werewolf."

"But I could."

"You could," he acknowledged.

Her toes started to itch. The pins-and-needles sensation from her arm jumped to her spine, rippling down her body in a liquid rush that made her gasp and arch. "Jay—"

He caught her by the shoulders and turned her to look at him. "What's happening, Eden?"

It should have been agony. His fingers brushed the flannel wrapped around her upper arm, and she whimpered. Not pain. Prickling. Wild sensitivity so severe she wrenched away and tore the makeshift bandage free.

Her fingers encountered sticky blood and unbroken skin.

Jay pulled her arm toward him and ran his fingers over her flesh. "This isn't possible."

She could feel the individual ridges of his fingerprints. Time seemed frozen, his stroking touch overwhelming. "Jay—Jay I don't feel okay. I don't feel real."

His fingertips settled over the pulse in her wrist. Then he drew away with a curse and whirled the vehicle in a tight U-turn. "We're going to my place."

Her heart was racing. She couldn't just feel it, she could *hear* it. Muscle constricting, blood rushing, the air rasping in and out of her lungs. The roar could have originated inside her, or it could have been the wind whipping by the missing door of the SUV.

The streetlights wobbled and danced, so she squeezed her eyes shut and groped for the seat and the door. Splaying her hands against something solid made it seem less like she was spinning. "What's happening to me?"

He cursed again. "Something that shouldn't be. Not yet, damn it."

Oh God. She was turning into a werewolf.

"Make it stop." When she clenched her fingers, her nails scraped over the seat so loudly her head throbbed. "Please. Please, Jay, I don't want to be a werewolf. I'm not strong enough."

"Yes, you *are*," he argued. The firm words brooked no argument, so certain she could feel them in her gut. The pinpricks up and down her spine eased as something warmer took their place. It melted the tension in her shoulders and trickled down, light and teasing enough to raise goose bumps.

Her nipples tightened. Arousal kindled, embarrassingly abrupt, and she pressed her thighs together. Jay was touching her everywhere and nowhere, stroking along her skin and inside her mind with an intimacy that made her squirm.

Not touch. Not sight or smell or taste, and definitely not a sound. She couldn't hear anything over the roar of the wind and her pounding pulse. But she could sense him, and she wanted to roll in him. Drown in him.

Then he did touch her, strong hands sliding over her back, under her legs. "Come on."

She jerked away, disoriented that he was reaching for her from the right. The seat beside her was empty and the SUV was parked. "Where are we?"

"My house." He lifted her in his arms and kicked the passenger door shut. "We've got to get you inside."

The world dipped again, and color exploded behind her eyes. Dazzling greens and vivid golds twisted and danced as she hid her face against his throat with a not very human whimper.

Jay pressed his lips to her temple and another wave of heat washed over her.

Stroking. Coaxing. He was surrounding her, pushing in from all sides, and some foreign part of her pushed back. The forces collided at her skin and sparked lightning. She cried out and struggled in his arms, driven by the sudden urge to fight, to flee, to *run*.

Another door slammed, and Eden felt cool wood under her hands. Jay was still whispering, only this time his fingers moved busily, tugging open the buttons on her shirt.

Good. Her shirt was claustrophobic. Clutching, clinging fabric, trapping her in her body. Her fingers felt too clumsy, but his glided over the buttons, freeing one after another with a gentle rasp of fabric over plastic.

Patient. She had to be patient. But when he slipped his hands under the fabric to guide it down her arms, he leaned close enough to put the vulnerable expanse of his throat at risk.

Clumsy, arrogant male. Snarling, she lunged for him, intent on setting her teeth in his skin.

He stopped her short with a firm hand wound in her hair. "Bite me and I'll spank you."

She panted, sucking in short, sharp breaths that only served to drag his scent into her lungs. She'd never noticed it

25

before, not really. Not enough to pick apart the clean smell of soap from the sharp undertones of his aftershave. And she'd never imagined the lower notes, the earth, the rain—like the wind when it ripped through town ahead of a bad storm. Wild nature, unchecked.

Seductive. She strained against his grip on her hair, yearning toward his throat with a different purpose now. To bury her face in the crook of his neck and wallow in that wildness, to rub her cheek against his skin so the intoxicating memory of it would linger after he was gone.

Instead of loosening his hold on her hair, he tugged her head back, baring the line of her throat. A brush of lips, almost like a kiss—and then he bit her.

She only had a moment to register the stinging pain of his teeth before satisfaction roared up to consume it. Every muscle in her body melted like warm taffy as the urge to fight him dissolved.

Quiet. So quiet. She almost remembered words. "Jay?"

"I'm here," he rasped. "I've got you." His hand dropped to her pants and pulled them open.

Human modesty slammed against the wall of madness, and she wriggled away with an alarmed noise. "What, why—"

He held up both hands. "If you don't get them off now, you'll get tangled up in them and freak out."

She couldn't make sense of the words, could barely understand them, but she understood the retreat in his upheld hands, the worry and care in his tone. Jay wouldn't hurt her. Closing her eyes, she eased out of her shoes, pants and underwear, tossing the clothing aside until she knelt shivering and naked on the hardwood floor.

He wrapped his arms around her and bit her again, this time a gentle press of teeth to the back of her neck. "Don't be afraid, and don't fight. Just feel her. Let her out."

The words vibrated through the room, a command and a soothing order, neither of which she knew how to obey. An anxious pressure built inside her, one uncomfortably like arousal. "Help. Help me."

"She's in there, honey, I know she is. Find her."

Her. The wild strangeness. Eden shivered. "She's calm now."

"Yeah." He stroked a hand over her hair.

She shivered again, only this time it didn't stop. Shivers turned to trembling, and trembling to shaking. The tension inside seized tight without warning, bowing her back as her nails scraped helplessly over the floor.

Pain shot down her spine. Bones cracked. Eden tried to scream and couldn't get enough air into her burning lungs. Her body tore apart in slick, wrenching agony.

Broken.

Dying.

No, not dying. Remade. Reborn. Power rode the pain, swelled and swelled until there was no way to contain the sweetness, the glory. Her wolf swept aside the last bit of human thought in a rush to claim her, and the sound of her own triumphant howl chased her into the wild.

Chapter Two

She was still sleeping.

Jay knelt on his bedroom floor and peered under the bed. "Eden? You awake?"

A muffled, sleepy noise answered him. Eden tried to curl onto her side and froze when her shoulder bumped the box spring. Her eyes snapped open. "Uh..."

He turned his head. "I brought you a shirt."

"All right," she said, voice faint. "Could—could you give me a minute?"

"Do you need me to do anything?" He'd left her alone for most of the night. After her change, no amount of comfort or soothing magic seemed to get through to her. She'd hidden under the bed, and Jay had slept on the floor beside it.

She squirmed a little and bit off a curse as something thudded against the bed frame. "Maybe lift the bed a little? This is awkward as a naked human."

"Yeah." Better to put his eyes above the mattress anyway. He rose on his knees, lifted the frame with one hand and held out the shirt with the other.

Her body brushed his as she crawled past him, grabbing the shirt on the way. By the time he lowered the bed, she'd tugged the garment over her head. "Thank you. Do I want to know how I ended up under there?"

"I think you wanted to den up and hide. It's pretty common after an initial change."

"So it wasn't a dream."

He turned to find her kneeling a few feet away on the floor, rubbing her cheek against the sleeve of the shirt he'd lent her. "No, not a dream," he whispered. It was too much for her to go through, for *anyone* to face. "I'm sorry."

She dragged in a shaky breath before burying her nose in the sleeve. "It smells like you. I don't even know how I know that, but it's comforting."

"Your sense of smell will be a lot more pronounced now." He could handle teaching, offering her information, and he knew a woman like Eden was bound to appreciate it. "People think wolves have the best sniffers out there, but it's not true, not compared to a lot of dog breeds. Sound, though—that's a big one. Your brain will block out the worst of it, but loud noises might be painful until you get used to them."

Her gaze dropped to his chest as her eyes narrowed. "I can hear your heart."

"You'll be able to see in the dark too." He rose and held out his hand. "Hungry?"

"Starving." She let him pull her to her feet but didn't release his hand. "Jay... Thank you for taking care of me."

His skin tingled at her touch. She'd slept two feet away from him, he'd seen her naked, and now she was wearing his shirt. Not just wearing, but *luxuriating* in, like his scent was the only thing she wanted on her body ever again.

He bit his tongue. Hard. "You're welcome."

She swayed toward him, like she was fighting the urge to close the distance between them. Her fingers clenched tight as she turned away. "I can feel her. She's me, but she's separate. And she's not confused."

"Good." Too many new wolves went nuts from the sudden shift in sensory input, not to mention the lifelong implications— the transformation was irreversible, those changes unavoidable. Adjusting was hellish, and some people couldn't do it at all.

If Eden was one of them…

It didn't bear consideration. Jay would have had to end her misery, and how the hell would he explain that to Zack? To Eden's father?

How would he handle it himself?

She cleared her throat. "Am I supposed to want to sniff you?"

"If you want to check me out." Only shit, that sounded like an invitation. "You're going to want to test other wolves. That's unavoidable."

Silence. Eden edged closer, as if she couldn't help herself, her gaze fixed on his throat. "If you don't want me to, I think you better run or lock me in the bathroom or something."

"Yeah? Well, I'm going to do neither," he answered. "I wish we had a couple of days for you to hide away from the world and deal with this, but we don't. We've got to get you solid on your feet and head back out to the farm."

She moved in a rush, slamming against his chest and burying her face in his throat with a distressed whimper. Her fingers dug into his shoulders in a painful grip that only eased after her first gasping breath.

Jay wrapped his arms around her, already regretting his blunt words. "Hey, you're okay. You're fine, Eden. Just fine."

"I know." The words sounded more frustrated than scared, but the nervous energy pulsing just under her skin didn't fade. "I don't have time to fall apart. I need to be stronger." She dragged in another breath. "Why do you smell so safe?"

"Because I'm strong. Because you know me already."

"Because I trust you?" She turned her cheek to his shoulder with a sigh. "Tell me I can do this, and I promise to believe you."

That much, at least, was easy. "I've seen people way weaker than you handle this. You can do it, no doubt at all."

"Okay." She eased out of his arms and glanced down at her bare legs. "I need food and clothes, and then we should get back out to the farm."

"Your clothes are in the bathroom." He dragged his gaze away from her legs and focused his mind on something else. "I made breakfast. You've probably already figured out what."

She tilted her head and narrowed her eyes. "Bacon and eggs? And coffee. Oh, thank *God*."

"Real cream too. I hate that powdered stuff." He gestured to the door. "I'll be in the kitchen, okay?"

She offered him a shy smile. "I'm fine. I have to be, right?"

"You're fine, Eden." He didn't have to dig deep to put the force of his conviction behind the words. "You're perfect."

"I bet you say that to all the women who sleep under your bed."

"Only the ones who blush as pretty as you." Then, before he could get himself into big trouble, he ducked out of the room.

The vehicles from Memphis were gone.

Jay pulled his truck to a stop in front of the farmhouse. "You think they parked the other cars out back?"

"Probably. Zack knows all about nosy neighbors."

They'd have to come up with a more permanent solution—once Jay knew what the hell was going on. "Hang on. It's an old truck, so I'll have to come and let you out." He climbed out and hurried around to open her door.

Eden slipped off the seat and stood next to him for a moment, her body tense as she took in the farm with her newly awakened senses. The front door slammed open, and she stumbled back against the truck.

Zack strode out the door and jumped the porch steps, landing a dozen yards in front of them. His nostrils flared as he stared at Eden. "What in—" His teeth snapped together as he found Jay's gaze, but the question remained, even if Zack seemed unwilling to frighten Eden by voicing it.

"Her bite healed right after we left," Jay told him quietly. "She shifted last night. I don't know how or why."

"Fucking hell." Zack ran both hands through his hair. "God, Eden, I'm sorry—"

"No." She straightened and gave Zack a stubborn look bristling with untamed challenge. "We're not doing this. It happened, it's over. Now we're going to go inside and discuss what's going on and what needs to be done."

Zack backed down. Judging from the raw, ragged power that spilled out of the man, he relented either out of respect for his cousin or because he was simply tired of fighting.

"We need the whole story," Jay said. "It's the only way I can help."

"Okay." Zack studied Eden for a moment longer before his lips quirked in an awkward, sad smile. "You weren't this bossy when you were ten."

"I was shorter too." She slipped her hand into Jay's. "Trust him, Zack. He's a good man. Whatever you guys are running from..."

"The same thing every other wolf is." Zack turned his back on them and started toward the porch. "Might as well come in. Waiting won't make it hurt less to hear. Or to say."

"Never does." Jay pocketed his keys and kept hold of Eden's hand as they followed her cousin up the steps and into the house.

Though he could hear plenty of footsteps and movement in the upstairs rooms, they didn't run into anyone as Zack led them to the kitchen. The girl who'd saved Eden the previous night was standing in front of the sink, and Zack's severe expression softened slightly. "Kaley, could you run and get Lorelei?"

Her gaze fell on Eden as she dried her hands, and her brow furrowed in confusion. "Uh...sure. She's just out back."

Jay watched her go. "How many of you are there?"

"Six, other than me." He sank into the chair like his whole body ached. "No—four. There was a couple expecting a baby, but they split after last night's attack. Now there's one other man and three women. Everyone's pretty roughed up."

Jay took the chair opposite his. "Your pack?"

He nodded, not looking at Eden. "Memphis is too big for only one. There was the strongest pack, but they always left the rest of us alone, as long as we paid our tribute."

"What changed?"

"The alpha let too many vicious bastards join up." Zack's features twisted into a scowl. "By the time he realized *how* vicious they were, it was too late. They put him down and turned Memphis into their playground."

An old story, the kind of thing that happened all too often. Especially in cities, where the stress of hiding amongst humans seemed to lead to ever-increasing savagery. "So you ran."

"Not at first." The words came from a slender blonde standing in the doorway. She walked in with a grave look at Zack. "Kaley wanted to come back, but I sent her out to the barn with Mae. I figured you wouldn't want her in here for this."

"Thank you." Zack cut a look at Eden. "You don't have to listen to this either, you know."

Eden stared right back. "I think I do. I'm a part of it, whether you want me to be or not, and I need as much information as I can get."

Zack smacked his hand on the table with a growl. "You don't get it, Eden. You don't know what life in a city is like for a

33

werewolf. In your worst nightmares, you can't imagine it." He gave Jay a desperate look. "You know I'm right."

"So is Eden. Like it or not, this is part of her life now." Jay laid his hand over hers. "But be sure you want to hear this, honey. You don't have to—not yet, anyway."

Eden squeezed his hand lightly, then pulled hers away and offered it to the blonde. "I'm Eden. You must be Lorelei."

The woman nodded but kept her hands to herself as she slid into the remaining empty chair. Eden let her hand fall to the table, her embarrassment plain.

Zack sighed and rubbed his face. "They asked me to step aside as alpha. When I didn't, they snatched me off the street and told my pack I was dead."

Lorelei took over. "With Zack gone, most of the stronger men tried to fight. They died. The ones who didn't took their loved ones and ran. With all the outward opposition gone, the gang pretty much did whatever the hell they wanted."

"But you weren't dead," Eden said softly.

"I wasn't dead," Zack agreed. "They were having too much fun beating the shit out of me."

If the fresh scars on the man's face, neck and arms were any indication, they'd done more than that. They'd tortured him, and with magically enchanted weapons, no less. It was the only thing Jay could think of that wouldn't heal, the reason he still had a shallow, scabbed-over scratch on his own side. "What about everyone else?"

"They hid. A few of us couldn't." Lorelei looked away. "It was bad, but nothing we couldn't get through. Not until Kaley—"

A surge of raw, angry power burst through the room. Zack clenched his jaw and his fists and *still* looked like he was about to punch a hole through the table.

Jay held up a hand. "It's okay."

Zack sucked in a steadying breath. "They didn't say as much in front of me, but I knew they'd go after the pack. It didn't matter how broken I was—I had to get free and get them the hell out of Memphis."

"So you left," Jay murmured. "But why did they follow? Could they want you all back that badly?"

"Last night was personal." Zack rose and retrieved a cloth-wrapped bundle from a drawer by the sink. He set it on the table before carefully pulling back the fabric to reveal a twist of herbs, twine and a lock of bright pink hair.

Jay picked it up and turned it over in his hands. "The girl from the woods. Mae."

"That's right." Lorelei leaned forward. "One of the new alphas—Scott Fields—he took a shine to her. At least, that's what we thought. Then he got...crazy. Plain old bugfuck insane."

Zack snarled. "He stalked her, is what he did. Tried to make her feel indebted by keeping the other men off her. And with no one to protect her, what the hell other choice did she have?"

He exploded from the table, toppling his chair to the floor. Furious, jagged power smashed through the room in a brutal wave. Lorelei sucked in a breath, and Eden jerked beside Jay, nervous ripples of magic vibrating off her.

If he didn't calm her down, she'd shift—suddenly and painfully. "That's enough," he said firmly. "Everyone *settle down.*"

Zack whipped around, his mouth open to deliver what would undoubtedly be a vicious retort, judging from the rage in his eyes. Then his gaze tripped over Lorelei and settled on Eden, who was practically hyperventilating, her fingers locked around the edge of the table.

He stumbled back and hit the wall with a hollow thud. "I can't do this. I can't take care of them."

Jay stood. "I'll help them in any way I can, but I can't do it alone."

Zack met his gaze. "Are there more of you in town? Do you have some sort of pack here?"

"No, there's just me."

Something deadly stirred behind the other man's gaze, a banked fury that eclipsed his previous anger and turned his next words into a venomous threat. "The only other alpha we have is Kaley, and she is *not* going to be your partner."

Jay held his gaze. "To be honest, I kind of figured she was with you."

That put an entirely different look in Zack's eyes. Panic. "She's not. But I'm responsible for her, just like I'm responsible for all of them."

And the weight of that responsibility would break him—sooner rather than later. "So let me handle it for a while. I've got the contacts, I know this place... It'll be easier."

Zack turned to Lorelei, who stared back at him, unblinking, and nodded once, almost imperceptibly.

The press of Zack's power melted away. "I yield. If Eden says I can trust you...then I yield."

"I'll need to call some friends. Will you be okay with that?"

"Are they friends who'll keep their hands to themselves?"

Jay ignored Eden's squeak of outrage. "Yeah, they are."

"Fine." Zack glanced at Lorelei again. "You can tell them everything they need to know," he growled before spinning out of the room. A few seconds later another door slammed shut.

Lorelei ran her hands through her hair. "Sorry. He's been through a lot."

"*I'm* sorry." Eden folded her hands on the table, her knuckles white. "You've all been through so much."

Jay had calls to make, and there were practical matters to deal with. "Lorelei, if you make a list of things you need—food, flashlights, sleeping bags, anything—I'll make sure you get them today. Tomorrow, we'll get started on things like electricity."

"There are immediate needs." She stood. "Zack said there are some things stored in the attic we might be able to use. I'd appreciate some help looking around, Eden."

Eden pushed out of her chair without meeting Jay's eyes. "I repacked a lot of it after my uncle died. I'll show you."

A mundane task, but it could be what she needed to keep going at the moment. "You'll be all right?" Jay asked.

She managed a half-smile. "I'll shout if I start sniffing people or going crazy again."

"Deal." He dug his cell phone out of his pocket and dialed as he stepped out onto the front porch.

Fletcher answered on the third ring. "That you, Ancheta?"

"It's me. You still in Nevada?"

"Nah, chased that prey to ground a month back. I'm enjoying the sun in Florida this week. Purely recreational."

"Where in Florida?" Neal Fletcher had nothing holding him, no reason not to pick up and head for west Tennessee. "Panhandle or down south?"

"Panhandle. Why, you got trouble up your way?"

"In a manner of speaking. A splintered pack of refugees out of Memphis just fell into my lap."

Fletcher spit out a curse. "Have you called Colin yet? Last time I talked to him, he mentioned checking out Memphis after he finished up his current gig. If it's bad enough to catch his attention, you're going to need more than me for backup."

Moira Rogers

"Alphabetical order in my contacts list, Fletch. First you, then Colin, and then Shane." He stepped off the porch and rounded the edge of the house. "What had Colin heard about Memphis?"

"Nothing good. A few of those bastards are into pain and tears. Enchanted blades and leaving their victims scarred up. Shit like that."

"Damn it." Jay had seen some of Zack's scars, but what others did he bear? And what about the rest of them? "It'll mean a fight. Are you up for it?"

"Sure. It'll take me a day or so to get on the road, but I owe you."

"Thanks, man." Jay ended the call with a deep breath and ticked one more thing off his mental list of things to do.

One down, way too many to go.

Eden opened the box marked *GG's china* and smiled as she lifted out a plate with a pattern of whimsical blue flowers encircling the rim. "Grandma Green's china. It would be nice to see it put to some use instead of gathering dust."

Lorelei peered over her shoulder. "Are you sure you want us using your grandmother's dishes? Wouldn't you rather take them home?"

"I have plenty crowding the house from the other side of the family already." Eden traced her finger over a flower. "I never knew Grandma Green, but Dad always said she was a practical sort of lady. No-nonsense. I bet she'd approve."

"Then we'll certainly put it to use." Lorelei dragged a hair elastic off her wrist and twisted her hair up into a high, sloppy ponytail. "We'll probably end up cooking in shifts just to feed everyone."

Easy to believe. Jay had shoveled three meals' worth of eggs and bacon onto Eden's plate that morning, and she was

38

hungry again. "So wanting to eat everything in sight isn't a temporary condition?"

"Not hardly. It's an enduring trait of your average werewolf."

"Damn." She put the plate back and lifted the box. Carefully. The first time she'd braced her weight to heft a box, she'd almost thrown it into her own face. "I guess I'll have to get used to it. And everything else."

Lorelei pulled open the folded flaps of another box. "I remember. It's crazy at first, but you acclimate faster than you might expect."

"Yeah?" Eden straightened and rubbed the back of her neck. "I don't remember changing. I remember being in Jay's car, and I think I remember trying to bite him. I woke up under his bed."

The other woman regarded her thoughtfully. "What do you remember most? Like, what feeling? Fear?"

Everything after the attack had melted into a disjointed blur, but one thing stood out. She brushed her fingers over the base of her neck and remembered Jay's teeth closing there, sending desire throbbing through her body.

Her cheeks heated. "No, not fear."

Lorelei shrugged. "Then it sounds like it could have been worse. You'll be all right."

She must sound spoiled and ungrateful to a woman who'd endured the sort of things Lorelei had. Eden bit back a self-conscious apology and turned to the next box. "I know I will. What I'm worried about is helping the rest of you be all right."

"You may as well pack it in right now, because the only thing that can do that is time."

"Then that's what we'll work for. Time." The next box held linens, each sheet individually folded and packed in its own plastic bag. Eden remembered folding them, remembered drowning her guilt over her lack of sorrow for her dead uncle in meticulous care for his belongings.

Fitted sheets had been a lot easier to care about than Zack's father.

Eden lifted one of the bags. "Sheets and blankets, though we'll need to round up some more furniture. But if Jay's willing to make a trip with me tonight, I can at least bring over a couple of twin beds and a futon mattress."

Lorelei caught her arm. "I didn't mean to sound ungrateful."

"No. God, no." Eden covered Lorelei's hand with her own. "This is hard. And awkward. It's the most confusing day of my life, and I wish I knew how to handle all of it better."

The woman stared down at the bagged sheet in Eden's hand. "One of them was going to rape her. Kaley. But he screwed up, started taunting her about how maybe he should do it in front of Zack instead. We all thought he was dead, and when Kaley heard that...she lost it."

Zack couldn't stand to listen. Eden had to. "What did she do?"

"She ripped his throat out," Lorelei whispered. "With her bare hands."

Eden was unprepared for the surge of brutal satisfaction. "Good," she rasped, her voice holding an edge of a snarl that shocked her out of the moment. "Oh hell, I didn't mean it like that."

"Why not?" Lorelei's smile was a little vicious, almost feral. "He was trying to hurt her. Worse, he was going to use her to hurt someone she cares about."

"Zack." Eden had heard his heart rate soar every time someone mentioned Kaley's name. She'd *felt* the deception, had almost been able to taste the lie in the air. No wonder she'd never been able to fool him during their childhood. "He was lying about her, wasn't he? Are they involved?"

"No, he wouldn't bring her down like that." Lorelei hesitated. "They hurt him, Eden. I mean, Zack had shit going on before—we all knew it—but this thing in Memphis? It almost broke him."

"This wasn't a happy place for him," Eden said carefully. Even brushing those memories kindled fierce anxiety in her gut, the terrifying pressure that made her feel like she no longer fit inside her own skin. "I can't imagine what he went through, but it must have been bad to drive him back here."

"Now you know. As much as I do, anyway. I figured you deserve that."

"Thank you." Eden shifted the box of linens to the stack going downstairs. "I need to get my dad out here. He was always the only person Zack would talk to."

Lorelei leaned back on her heels. "He knows, right? About the werewolf thing?"

"About Zack? Yeah." Eden smiled wanly. "About me? No, not yet."

"But you can tell him." The other woman's smile matched hers. "I'm a little jealous."

Yet another way she was lucky. "Once he gets done shaking me, he'll probably spend his free time over here feeding you all until you hate the sight of food."

"It'd take a while." Lorelei's smile faded slowly. "Jay. How long have you known him?"

"Four—no, five years?" Eden narrowed her eyes and tried to remember. Jay had arrived in town a few years after she'd come back from college, replacing the old Chief of Police at his retirement. "I haven't known him well for that whole time, but he's in my dad's diner pretty much every day."

"You trust him."

It wasn't a question, but Eden still answered it without hesitation. "With my life."

"Okay." Lorelei looked away. "I don't want to have to worry about his friends, but...it's exactly the way the alphas in Memphis took over, you know? None of them were strong enough to stand alone, so they banded together. I don't think I can help being a little nervous."

A different sort of pressure built inside Eden. An ache just below her breastbone, one that blossomed in reaction to Lorelei's slumped shoulders and tired eyes. She took a step forward, then another, watching Lorelei for any sign that the woman was about to retreat.

She started to raise her arm, but froze when she caught the slight stiffening in the other woman's shoulders. "I'm sorry," she said softly, letting her arm fall back to her side. The pressure became pain, glass shards in her throat, and she had to force each word out carefully. "If there's anything I can do to make it easier for you and your friends, tell me. I'll tell Jay to keep his friends away from the farm for a while, if that's easier."

"No," Lorelei said forcefully. "I just wanted you to know. So you could understand. But we'll all deal with it, I promise."

She wanted to snarl that none of them should *have* to deal with anything right now. But if Eden pressed the issue, Lorelei might not be as ready to confess to other worries and fears. "Okay," she said instead, trying to silence her newly awakened wolf's agitation. "What about the others? Are there any in particular who need to be given some space?"

"Mae. Without question."

The one who'd been stalked. Eden rubbed a hand over her arm as a chill shivered through her. "The man who hurt her. He was one of the ones who came here last night?"

"He was." Lorelei turned back to the box and began unpacking the rest of it, then continued matter-of-factly. "Don't worry. He's dead now."

The pressure intensified into a nagging tickle, and Eden scratched at her arm, wondering how the *inside* of her skin could itch. "Does she need attention? I have a friend in the next town over, someone with counseling training."

"That's nice of you to think of, but I don't think it would help. There's so much—" Lorelei's voice cracked, and she swallowed hard. "There's a lot she couldn't talk about. The worst things, in some ways."

The memory rose in spite of Eden's best efforts to hold it at bay, vivid in the way it replayed itself in her nightmares. Zack, seventeen and shirtless, with the height of a man but the build of an underfed teen. She could still smell the rain, hear the thunder that accompanied each flash of lightning.

She would never forget the sight of him, shirtless and bleeding, his back torn up by his father's belt but already healing. The rain washed away the blood, and by morning there was no proof of the way Albus Green beat the hell out of his kid. No marks, no witnesses.

No one but her. Gawkish, terrified Eden, nine years old and rendered mute by the promise he'd extracted from her so many years ago she couldn't remember not having made it. The defining rule of her childhood, the Green Rule. *Don't tell anyone.*

Eden's arm itched. Burned. She dug her fingers into her skin, the metallic scent of blood a welcome distraction from the nightmares. "I understand," she told Lorelei in a voice that didn't sound like hers. Too distant. Too calm.

Lorelei's hand settled over hers. "You're bleeding."

Pull yourself together, Eden. She gathered every scrap of willpower she'd ever called hers and pushed the power of her wolf into an angry, painful knot in her chest. It made every breath hurt, but it allowed her to smile and pull her hand from her arm. "I was always bad at scratching things that itch. You should have seen me with the chicken pox."

"Okay." Lorelei rose and wiped her hands on her jeans. "I need to make out that list for Jay. Do you want to come with me?"

Eden didn't itch anymore. She hurt, like her wolf was clawing up the inside of her skin, trying to get out.

As long as the pain stayed internal, she could hide it.

She leaned down and hefted the box of china. "Absolutely. Some stuff we'll have to buy, but I might have a lot of it in my house or in storage. My mom's family were a bunch of packrats."

"We'll figure it out. We always do."

With all of the advantages she'd been given, Eden could do nothing less. She wouldn't allow herself to consider any alternative.

Chapter Three

"I'm just saying, I wouldn't have paid for it myself." Louis Stevens leaned back in his chair.

Jay spared his deputy a glance as he searched through a stack of files on his desk. "It was my fault. Why shouldn't I pay for it?"

"It's a service vehicle, that's why."

"We're underfunded, Lou." And the detached door, deep scratches and bullet holes were better dealt with by another werewolf. "Besides, my guy down in Dyersburg knows his shit. He's kept my old truck running this many years."

"That *is* impressive." Lou snorted and swiveled his chair from side to side. "At least the deer got a happy ending."

"She'll live to graze another day." Jay straightened and stretched his back. "Are you sure you and Baker'll be able to handle it for a week without me?"

"Heck, yeah." Lou reached for his coffee. "You going to actually do something exciting with your time off? Baker thinks you spend your vacations studying how to be a better cop."

"I'm helping a friend move." It was as close to the truth as his coworkers would get. "I've got a few projects to work on around the house too."

"That's grim, man. No wild parties? No exotic vacations?" Lou grinned over the rim of his mug. "No sexy librarians?"

Obviously, Jay hadn't hidden his interest in Eden as well as he'd thought. But he was bound to be spending time with her around town, so better to get it out of the way now. "I'm thinking of asking her out, so keep your eyeballs to yourself."

"You got it, Chief." Though he tried, the deputy couldn't hide his smirk. "So if you two hook up, can you get her to forget my late fees?"

"Return the movies on time. Problem solved." Jay found the file he wanted and snatched it up.

Lou eyed the folder. "You're not taking work home, are you? Sort of defeats the purpose of a vacation."

"Nah, it's something personal."

"If you say so." He rose and held up his cup. "I'm getting more coffee. You want some?"

"No, I've got to run. Thanks, though." The bell above the door jingled as Jay pushed through it. The morning sun stung his eyes, and he dropped his sunglasses from the top of his head down onto the bridge of his nose as he made his way to his truck.

He slid behind the wheel and took a bracing breath before flipping open the manila folder. Inside lay a patchwork picture of anger, violence and resentment.

The first reports were spotty, neighbors phoning in disturbance calls when Albus and Kathy Green's arguments devolved into screaming matches. Eventually, the complaints coalesced into a steady stream of reports—most made by Eden's mother against her brother-in-law.

The file also told Jay when Kathy Green had left her family. Her departure marked the beginning of a clear pattern of neglect for Zack. Fights at school, a shoplifting complaint from the local grocer where the boy had been stealing food. Notes regarding an investigation by Child Protective Services.

What could they have found? Even a viciously beaten young werewolf would heal in less than eight hours. No bruises, no marks, nothing to hint at the pain.

Jay had seen a different sort of pain in Eden's eyes—the helpless kind that came from *knowing*.

His cell phone rang. He answered it absently, his eyes still fixed on a transcript from a 911 call. "Ancheta."

Eden's voice spilled out in a terrified whisper. "Jay? I need help."

He straightened and tossed the file aside. "What's wrong?"

"I can't breathe. I can't—" A raspy noise followed by a groan. "I was in a budget meeting and I lost my temper. Just *lost* it, and I feel like I'm being torn up from the inside."

His hand trembled, and it took him two tries to shove the key into the ignition. "You're at the library?"

"Yes. In my office. I had to use my cell phone and earpiece to call you. I broke my office phone when I picked it up."

"Don't move, and don't open your door. I'll come up the back exit and get you, okay?"

"Okay. Thank you. Thank you, Jay."

He pulled out onto the street. "Don't thank me. Just breathe, and I'll be there in a few minutes."

She let out a choked little laugh. "My coworkers have to think I was drinking at lunch. I acted crazy."

"Stress." Jay slowed at a red light, and was just about to roll through it when it turned green again. "They'll chalk it up to you working too hard."

"Maybe." Eden's voice dropped to a whisper. "Or they'll find out Zack's back in town and blame it on him."

"I won't let them do that. Anyone who has a problem with your family can come to me."

He had to listen to a few of her short, pained breaths before she spoke again. "Is there something wrong with me? Should I be able to handle this?"

"There's nothing wrong with you." But she would need to hear more. "Some people handle the transformation like it's nothing, and other folks never get a handle on it. You're doing good, Eden."

"I'm not doing enough. Lorelei... She *hurts*, Jay. She hurts so much, and I'm not helping. I think that's why I can't breathe. I'm so angry."

Jay cursed silently. There was precious little he could do for Eden from behind the wheel of his speeding truck. "It'll be better once the full moon is past."

"Okay. Okay, I can make it that long." Something clattered in the background. "I can even—"

"Eden?" His phone beeped as it dropped the call, and he threw it on the seat with a vicious curse. "*Fuck.*"

He should have kept her with him. He should have warned her that maybe she should stay out at the farm, take some time off. Anything to keep her from hiding in her office, cowering like a hurt animal.

He'd fucked up, and now he could only hope Eden didn't suffer for it.

He pulled onto the narrow street behind the library and braked hard, his truck coming to a halt with a shuddering screech. He couldn't go up the side stairs without someone seeing, so he jumped up, grabbed hold of the ladder to the fire escape and pulled it down.

The noise must have roused Eden. By the time he reached her window, she was struggling to open it, her teeth cutting into her lower lip as she concentrated on turning the locks like it was the hardest task she'd ever set for herself. "I broke the phone," she said as she eased the sash up with shaking hands. "I'm afraid to touch anything."

No time to climb inside, not with her eyes so wild and her skin burning. Jay grasped her hands to his chest. "Look at me, Eden Green. Now."

The command stirred her wolf. Power gathered beneath her skin, all that wildness finding a focus in challenging him. Eden's gaze snapped to his, her blue eyes already melting to glowing gold.

He cupped the back of her head and dragged her mouth to his.

A growl worked up her throat, low and warning, but in the next second her mouth opened under his. She slapped both hands to his shoulders, dragging him closer.

Arousal, intense and instantaneous. Jay took the invitation of her open mouth, sliding his tongue over hers before nipping at her lower lip. She whimpered and tilted her head, chasing his tongue with hers. Her fingernails dug into his back as she pressed against his chest.

Her nipples were hard. Without thinking, he cupped her breast through her shirt and rubbed his thumb over the taut peak.

She moaned and arched her back, pushing her breast closer to his hand. Her mouth tore free of his, and she dropped her head back, offering her throat in a moment of unrestrained hunger.

Jay leaned in and shuddered to a stop a heartbeat before closing his teeth on her skin. "Eden."

Her breath whistled out through her teeth. "Oh my God."

Too far. Too much. Belatedly, he snatched his hand away. "Sorry."

"I should be." Shivering, Eden dropped her forehead to his shoulder. "But that was a very efficient distraction."

He'd meant it to be, before the taste of her had overwhelmed his better sense. "Good," he muttered. "That's good."

Her shoulders shook with her restrained laugh. "Do you, uh, want to come in? This is a little Romeo and Juliet right now, and that doesn't tend to end well."

"Got it." Her hair was soft, and he couldn't resist stroking his fingers through it. "Want to get out of here?"

"Yes," she said without hesitation. "God, yes. I can't concentrate, I'm exhausted..."

"If I'd explained all this better, you might have called in sick."

Eden eased back and gave him an amused look. "How long have you known me?"

Long enough to know she took about as many days off work as he did. "Fair enough."

"I'm stubborn to a fault, I know that." She turned, slipped on her jacket and dumped her cracked cell phone into her purse. "But I try to learn from my mistakes."

"Still, maybe you and Zack should talk to your father tomorrow instead of this afternoon."

"Maybe." She eyed the office door, then him. "Are you spiriting me out the window?"

Her barely concealed glee drew his first real smile since finding out what had happened in Memphis. "What, you want to sneak down the fire escape like a teenager?"

She actually blushed as she swung her purse over her shoulder. "It would be the most impulsive thing I've ever done in my life. And probably the most romantic too."

"Then come on." He grasped her hand. "We can head to the farm, or even go hide somewhere. Lady's choice."

The sparkle in her eyes faded a little. "Going to the farm would be the right thing. They need help more than I do."

That dimming light made his chest ache. "That's crap, Eden. What do *you* need?"

"I need to help them." She squeezed her eyes shut and pressed one hand against her chest. "Yesterday, when I was in the attic with Lorelei... God, the shit that's happened to them. I could feel her pain like it was my own—worse, even. I don't want to feel it again, but..." She opened her eyes and gave him a helpless look. "I need to fix it for her."

"It's what being alpha is about," he whispered. "But you can't fix things for her any more than I can. Any more than we can fix Zack."

"Alpha?" She rubbed at her breastbone with her fingertips, as if the ache lingered. "Is that what I am? Like you and Zack and Kaley?"

There were a hundred shades of it, a thousand ways to feel the power and responsibility of the relative position. "You need to take care of your pack."

"I do." She took his hand again and rested her knee on the windowsill. "I can't hide. I have to meet Zack and my dad. Zack needs it."

And the longer they waited to tell Austin the news, the worse he was bound to take it. "Your dad does too."

"Yeah." She slipped out the window to stand next to him on the narrow fire escape, so close she only had to sway forward to lean against his chest. "Will you stay close by, in case this happens again?"

It felt selfish, even if it *was* practical. "We should plan on staying together for the next few weeks—if you're okay with that."

Her fingers tightened in his shirt. "I should have gone home with you last night when you asked me. I don't think I slept at all."

"So now we know. Your place or mine? Or the farm?"

"Not the farm," she said quickly. "I don't know if I'd sleep much better out there, even with you around."

"My house?"

"Sure." She rubbed her cheek against his shoulder once and sighed as she pulled away. "Want to go over to the diner now? It's a little early, but I'm hungry." She made a face. "Again."

Jay swung down onto the ladder. "May as well eat before Austin hands the grill over to Gary for the afternoon. Damn kid can't cook."

"He's getting better," Eden chided. "Papaw always said Dad was a disaster in the kitchen when he started out too. Gary will learn."

"Uh-huh." Jay covered the last bit of distance with a jump and reached up to steady Eden. "All the same, an early lunch sounds good to me. Then I can make myself scarce while you take care of business."

When she had both feet on the ground, she stared back up at her window, her expression caught between amusement and awe. "Does being a werewolf make you less clumsy? I think I would have broken a leg trying to climb down that thing in my heeled boots last week."

"It's not all bad, especially once you get used to it." He looped an arm around her shoulders and felt a little of his own stress melt away at her proximity. "Come on, let's go eat."

The diner had mostly cleared out by one-thirty. At a quarter to two, Eden slipped into the kitchen and smiled at her father. "Can Gary spare you for an hour so we can go upstairs and talk?"

Austin Green wrapped his gnarled fingers around his favorite coffee mug and leveled a stare at her. "Probably. What's all this about?"

Gary was pretending not to listen as he scraped a spatula over the griddle, so Eden tilted her head toward the back stairs. "Family stuff."

"You gonna tell me you and the chief are courting? Because I have eyes."

Her cheeks flamed. Gary smirked, but wiped the expression off his face when he glanced up and caught her furious glare.

Her dad stood there watching her over his coffee mug like she was still fifteen and owed him an answer. "It's not about that," she ground out. "It's about Zack."

Austin straightened and nodded toward the back staircase. "Have you heard from him?"

"Yes. But it's complicated." She climbed the narrow stairs behind him, skipping the creaky fifth step out of habit. Everything was familiar and new at the same time, the memories of her childhood a ghostly echo under the sharply focused version provided by her newly honed senses.

She'd already learned that the quickest way to go crazy was by concentrating on the details, so she fought to block them out as she followed her father into the apartment over the diner. "Zack's at the farm."

"Since when?" he asked sharply. "And why am I hearing about it like this?"

Fast was the only way to do it. Fast and brutal, and Eden allowed herself only one terrified moment to wonder if she'd still have a father before blurting out the truth. "Because I was attacked by a wolf at the farm two nights ago. A werewolf from Memphis who was there to hurt Zack. And I—I changed. Like Zack does."

The mug slipped from his fingers and shattered on the floor. "You what?"

Eden flinched. "I'm sorry. I didn't know how else to say it."

He waved away the words and stepped over the broken mug to grasp her shoulders. "Are you all right?"

The painful knot beneath her heart loosened for the first time in two days. Her father wasn't Zack's father. He would never hate her for a twist of fate beyond her control. "I'm okay," she whispered. "I'm okay, because Jay—Chief Ancheta—he's like Zack too. That's why he's here. He helped me."

Her father stared at her, an expression of helpless confusion twisting his features. "You're a wolf now. And so is the chief."

The urge to soothe him pulsed with every beat of her heart. Not as strong as with Lorelei, but undeniable. "I'm okay," she said again, putting force into her voice. She caught his hands and pulled him toward the dining room table. "Jay's not going to let anything happen to me. He likes your cooking too much."

Her father took a deep, shuddering breath. "Where is Zack? I want to see him."

"He's on his way over." Eden caught his hands. "Dad, he's hurt bad. Whatever happened in Memphis, it broke him."

"Worse than living with Albus?"

Eden swallowed hard and closed her eyes. "I'm pretty sure they tortured him."

Austin sighed, heavy and tired. "The last time I heard from him, he said things were okay. That he was doing fine."

The wolves who had fled Memphis with Zack seemed to care about him. Maybe he *had* been okay, before it all went to hell. "It was a werewolf thing. Almost like a war. Zack and his"—she had to stop stumbling over the word—"pack. Everyone who survived came here. Jay thinks he can take care of them, but I don't know if anyone can take care of Zack. I don't know if he'll let them."

He shook his head. "Zack's alive. I don't care what's been done to you, how you've been hurt, as long as you're living, you can heal."

"He's family, right?" Eden concentrated as she clutched her father's hands, too aware of the broken phone in her purse. A moment of temper, a spike of panic, and she could crush his fingers. "We can help him."

"Well, of course." His brow furrowed. "You said he brought others with him. Do they need anything?"

A tiny part of her wanted to throw the whole mess in his lap. Pretend she believed her father could fix anything, maybe pretend she'd ever believed it. God knew he'd always tried.

He'd never stop trying. That was what mattered. "Yeah, they need a lot. Food, furniture and supplies. I thought we could open up our old house. Some of Jay's friends are coming in from out of town to help."

"It might need some work—cosmetic things, mostly—but I don't see why not."

She heard heavy footsteps on the stairs and leaned in to hug her father. "Thank you, Dad. For not freaking out."

A shadow of pain sparked in his eyes. "I wouldn't, Edie. You're my *child*. That could never change."

"I know," she lied, glad he couldn't hear the tremor under the words. "Zack's coming up the stairs. Are you ready to see him?"

He rose and slid his shaking hands into his pockets. "You bet."

Zack's knock was almost tentative. When her father didn't move, Eden rose and pulled open the door with a wide smile. "Come on in. I was just about to ask Dad to make coffee."

Zack took one look at her father and frowned. "You already told him."

"Yeah."

"Oh." He looked past her to Austin. "I never wanted her to get hurt. If I'd known, I would have taken them somewhere else."

If the words registered, her father showed no sign. Instead, he walked up to Zack, his faded blue gaze taking stock of every scar, every line on his nephew's face. Then he lifted a hand, patted Zack's cheek and pulled him down into a hug.

Eden held her breath as Zack stood there, stiff and awkward in the embrace of a man who had never really been related to him—not by blood, anyway, even if Zack looked more like Austin than Eden ever had. But the bonds of their sad, broken little family had never rested on blood.

Austin clutched Zack to his chest like a long-lost son, and Zack's reserve melted under it. After an eternity, he lifted his arms and hugged the older man back, that tired, tentative gesture alone enough to make Eden's eyes burn. She turned away and hurried into the kitchen, covering her tears under the mundane task of making coffee.

Zack was alive. His so-called father was dead. The ghosts of Green Pines couldn't hurt him anymore, and Jay and his friends would make sure the same was true of whatever ghosts had followed from Memphis.

After so many years of secrets and suffering, maybe the Green family could finally start to heal.

Chapter Four

By the time Jay pulled his beat-up old truck into his driveway, Eden thought the short walk to the front door might be more than she could manage. Not physically—her body still thrummed with enough inexhaustible energy to leave her fidgeting, but her mind and heart hadn't caught up.

Or maybe being a werewolf only made your body stronger. Maybe the rest of her would never catch up, and she'd be a battered, stunted soul in a too-healthy body.

Like Zack, whispered a traitorous inner voice. *Like Lorelei and Mae.*

Eden pushed the thought away and waited for Jay to kill the engine before grabbing his hand. Touch rooted her now, like hopping onto a steady rock while the ground around her turned to quicksand. The darker thoughts melted away, replaced by her own attraction and the wolf's more cunning interest.

"How are you holding up?" he asked softly.

"I don't know." She ran her thumb over the back of his hand, savoring the heat of him, the way even the barest brush of skin felt illicit. Intimate. "I needed to get away from the farm again…but I still feel selfish for coming back here with you."

"We can be there in a matter of minutes if anything happens. Zack has my number."

She knew. Just as she'd known she'd reached her limit when Mae had snapped at one of the men over something tiny and foolish, her snarling tone more like a wounded animal's than a human's. The need to soothe her throbbed at the base of

Eden's skull like a migraine waiting to split wide open, but her attempts to reach out to the girl only provoked more fear.

Time. They all needed it, and no one knew if there would be enough. "Does it get easier? Not being able to help them, I mean. Not being able to make them feel safe."

He hesitated, and she realized he was thinking of doing it to *her* right now, thinking of lying to make her feel better. But finally he said, "No. The only thing you can do is try to make a safe place, and that's what we're going to do."

If Lorelei's pain stuck in Eden's throat like shards of glass, what was her own agony doing to Jay? She shifted on the bench seat, easing close enough to touch his jaw with her free hand. "Does that mean I'm hurting you?"

"No, nothing like that." He covered her hand with his and smiled faintly. "I just know how you feel, that's all."

"Good." She smoothed her thumb over his lower lip and remembered what it had felt like to kiss him. Hot and heady, every sense alive and screaming for more. More touch, more taste...more skin. "I feel safe right where I am. Confused as hell, but safe."

His smile grew, and he reached down to retrieve the grocery bag from the floorboard beside her feet. His arm brushed her leg as he moved, and his smile faded as he straightened. "You never said how it went today. Breaking the news to your father."

"He coped." Jay's throat had been so close to her mouth that she could have bitten it. Sank teeth into skin, left a bruise. A territorial statement she wasn't brazen enough to make with words. The thought intoxicated her, and she stumbled over her next words. "He, uh, he was more worried about Zack than me, I think. Zack looks worse off..."

"Looks can be deceiving." Jay dipped his head and caught her gaze. "Eden?"

His eyes were gorgeous. Dark and warm. "Yeah?"

His fingers brushed her cheek. "Come inside. I'll make dinner, and you can relax."

She realized she was swaying closer to him when her lips bumped his palm. She froze, her mouth parted on his skin, torn between the urge to lick or bite and the knowledge she *had* to pull back.

Not like this, in the front seat of his truck. She closed her eyes and eased away. "I'm sorry. I'm having trouble with the concept of personal space right now."

"You might for a while yet, but I'll try not to lean on you if I can help it."

Eden opened her eyes with a frown. "Lean on me?"

"Push you," he explained. A moment later, a swell of *something* filled the space between them, a call and a warning all wrapped up in one.

She almost rolled to her back with a whimper. A growl worked its way up her throat as her wolf fought the urge, leaving her torn between conflicting needs—test him by meeting challenge with strength, or fold and beg for the safety of his protection.

Eden made the choice before her wolf could, ducking her head and burying her face against his chest with a choked groan. "I don't think I'm a very smart wolf."

He tangled his fingers in her hair. "You're new, honey. Cut yourself some slack."

His chest was solid under her cheek. His hand in her hair tugged just enough to be a quiet show of dominance, one edged in sensual promise. She swallowed hard and wet her suddenly dry lips. "Is this how werewolves flirt?"

"Better than having to sniff someone's ass, isn't it?"

It startled a laugh out of her. "In most circumstances, I imagine."

"Mmm." He rattled the bag. "Steak. You haven't lived until I've grilled one for you, and that's a verifiable fact."

Steak sounded delicious enough to set her stomach to rumbling, but when she lifted her head, Jay's fingers stayed tangled in her hair. The pull was a different sort of delicious, dark and hot, and she caught his gaze as he freed her with teasing slowness.

He released her with a half-smile. "Fair warning. I'm going to kiss you again tonight...but not just yet."

Her heart skipped a few beats out of sheer glee. "I'd warn you about what I'm going to do in response, but I can't tell if my inner wolf will pick a fight with you or try to tear your clothes off. Probably one of those two, though."

"Finding out is half the fun." Then he pushed open his door and slid out of the truck.

She tugged absently at her own door handle, transfixed by the fantasy of wrestling to see who would come out on top. She forgot that the passenger door only worked from the outside until Jay pulled it open for her.

Eden stared at him for a moment before easing off the seat, clutching her overnight bag. "I didn't know you could cook," she said, carefully picking a topic that wouldn't involve either of them naked and rolling on the ground.

"I can—badly," he confessed as he laid his hand on her elbow. "But open flame and I get along really well."

"I'm hopeless. The family skill in the kitchen must have skipped my generation."

Jay led her around the side of the house to the back door. "I survive on breakfast foods and eating out. Aside from the steak, you've already tasted the best I have to offer."

"You probably help keep my dad in business some months." She stepped through the back door and hesitated just inside. This was a warning Jay deserved. "He's got some ideas about you and me. He might decide to have a talk with you."

Jay followed her across the threshold. "You've been staying at my house, spending all sorts of time with me. Of course he's got ideas."

Eden dropped her bag on the couch and sank beside it with a relieved sigh. "Don't let him nag. I'm a grown woman, and he has to get used to that."

Jay laughed as he set the grocery bag on the counter. "How do you know he's not going to tell me how pleased he is we're an item?"

If anyone could sidestep her father's grumpy disapproval, it would be the Chief of Police. "I bet you charmed all your girlfriends' parents growing up. Or were you not always this responsible and upstanding?"

"Not by a long shot." He pulled a glass dish from a cabinet and began to gather items from the refrigerator. "I was quite the hellion, actually. Into all sorts of stupid shit."

"So you started out a bad boy and ended up a cop?"

His expression sobered. "I managed not to run afoul of the authorities, but one night I wound up on the wrong end of a bad fight. A local pusher who used half-feral werewolves as muscle."

Oh, God. "How old were you?"

"Twenty-two."

Barely more than a kid. " Did you find someone to help you?"

"Yeah." His gaze lost focus, as if he was looking at something very far away. "They left me in an alley, and I would have died if Murray hadn't found me. He was an old wolf by then—older than I knew, probably. Practically lived on the streets."

Eden shivered in spite of the warmth of the room. "I think I must have had it easier than anyone."

"I don't know." He shook his head as if to clear it and laid the steaks in the glass dish. "There's no such thing as easy. There's only the difference between problems that are obvious and the ones that are hidden, right?"

She was an expert in the hidden problems. Not just an expert, but a conspirator in keeping them hidden, a thought grim enough to drive her off the couch in search of a distraction. "Can I help with anything?"

"Salad?" He gestured to the counter beside him, and his voice softened. "I looked at the reports, Eden. The paperwork on the complaints and investigations. It's all pretty clear, especially if you know *why* they never found any evidence of injuries on your cousin."

Eden froze halfway to the kitchen, her first reaction one of overwhelming, irrational panic. Anger followed hard on its heels, an outraged sense of betrayal and exposure. "You looked at my family's records?"

"I did," he said evenly.

She bit back her gut response. *You had no right.* He was putting his life and his reputation on the line to clean up her family's mess. Of course he had the right. But it didn't make her feel any less naked. All the lies, all the practice putting on a bright smile and pretending everything was okay—gone. Swept away in the space of a heartbeat.

He *knew.*

Anxiety prickled over her skin. "You could have asked me," she managed finally, rasping words that sounded so wounded to her own ears. "I would have told you." Those words sounded like a lie.

"I think you would have wanted to," he countered. "But old habits die hard. Trust me, I know."

Yes, they did. She laughed, short and bitter. "Yeah. I have a history of lying to the authorities about the subject, don't I?"

"That isn't what I mean. You were a *kid*, Eden."

She had to open her eyes. Face her shame, face the too-strong wolf who felt like an enemy right now. "I was a kid who knew what was happening, and I lied. I lied for years, and Zack's sorry excuse for a father beat the skin off his back more nights than not."

Jay abandoned the marinade and held his arms open. "Come here."

She wanted to. God, she wanted to. His embrace looked like safety and comfort rolled into one, but her feet were rooted in place, her entire body tensed to give in to the wolf and flee. "I don't know if I can."

He dropped his arms with a nod. "I could tell you the rest of my secrets, if it helps."

"You don't understand." She wiggled her fingers and rocked forward, testing the wolf's resolve. Her conflicting emotions only ratcheted the pressure higher. "I want to come there. I just...think I'm about to bolt."

"I know, but I'm not about to push you."

She snarled before she could stop herself, hot temper rising as fast as it had in the library. "This would be easier if you weren't so fucking *honorable*."

His lips twitched, and he cleared his throat. "You want me to take charge," he murmured, a thread of steel creeping into his voice. "And I will. When I know you're not just rolling over under me because you don't know anything else to do."

In a heartbeat, she crowded into his space, pressed close with a challenging growl. "Rolling under you is not my first instinct right now." Climbing him like a tree and riding him to the floor, on the other hand...

He slid his fingers into her hair again. "Do you know why you like this, honey? It's the control. You think you want it, but you don't. Just the fight. You still want me to win."

The words resonated, but she wasn't about to admit as much. "That doesn't sound very progressive of me. Don't werewolves get to have feminist pride?"

"Who said you aren't proud?" His gaze warmed as it traveled over her face. "You're amazing, Eden. After what happened to you, you could have given up. But you came up fighting instead."

She'd been joking, but the sincerity in his words made her self-conscious. Dropping her gaze, she traced a finger along the neckline of his T-shirt. "Maybe that's just luck. Whatever made me turn early and made me a powerful wolf. If it wouldn't hurt more, I think I'd still be whimpering under your bed."

The pulse throbbing at the base of his throat sped at her touch. "Hiding? Not you, no way."

"You'd be surprised." Edging her finger up a fraction allowed her to touch skin, and she hissed out a breath and jerked away as desire jolted through her. "Would you have asked me out if you'd known I knew about werewolves? Or is this all just because I am one now?"

"I would've." He smoothed his hands down to her shoulders. "I wasn't about to start something based on a lie, that's all."

That was how every relationship in her life had felt. "It's not easy. Even when the lie's not yours."

"Doesn't matter now." He stepped closer, looming over her. "Nothing else to hide."

Her insides were melting. She'd screwed around with enough guys in college to know she'd like giving up control to him when the time came—

When the time came. "Is this the part where you handcuff me to something?"

He bent his head and kissed her, his tongue edging her lips apart as soon as his mouth met hers. Nothing tentative this time, just an unrelenting kiss, deep and a little rough, and she rocked up on her toes and shoved her fingers into his hair to drag him closer.

His tongue slid over hers, and a moan vibrated deep in his chest. Only a moment later, he broke the kiss and rested his forehead on hers. "This...is where we have dinner."

The world was still spinning in lazy circles, but all the built-up tension had vanished. "How do you keep doing that?" she whispered. "She twists up inside me until I think I'm going to pop, and you make it all go away with a kiss."

"Don't know." A low chuckle escaped him. "Talent?"

"Maybe." She rubbed her cheek against his. "I don't know werewolf rules, but if we're not having a—a *thing* here, you'd better tell me now. I'm feeling territorial."

"Dinner," he said again, firmly this time. "The rest is up to us."

It wasn't enough of an answer to satisfy her, but it didn't look like she'd be getting a better one. Biting back a sigh, she stepped away. "You said you wanted me to make a salad?"

"Unless you want to go strictly carnivore tonight."

"That is uncomfortably appealing."

He grinned. "Do we dare?"

The smile was infectious. Eden laughed as she rolled up her sleeves to wash her hands. "No. I need something to do while you're burning meat."

Jay clucked his tongue and shook his head. "Always a good girl, huh?"

"Don't taunt me, Chief Ancheta." She lowered her voice to a husky promise. "I might decide to try my hand at naked cooking."

He passed her a bamboo cutting board and pulled a knife free of the block. "Sounds kinky."

"Maybe I am kinky." She eyed the knife with a grin. "Not *that* kinky. But I do work in the building with all the books, even dirty ones. Good luck shocking me."

"I wouldn't dream of trying, Ms. Green. Not for a moment."

Jay woke with a start. He watched the ceiling fan turn slow revolutions above him, every sense on high alert.

In his bedroom, Eden whimpered, a sound cut short by a sharp gasp. He shot off the couch, kicking away the blanket that tangled around his legs.

She was staring at the ceiling, wet lines of tears tracking down her face to disappear in the damp hair at her temples. Jay knelt by the bed. "Eden? What happened?"

She wiped at her cheeks with trembling hands. "Nothing. Just...dreams."

Nightmares. "What do you need?"

"I was going to turn the lights on, but I guess I don't need them anymore." She reached for him with one hand. "You were right. I can see in the dark."

"It takes some getting used to." He tucked her hand between his. "Family stuff?"

Eden wiped at her cheek again with a watery little laugh. "I guess that's where it all comes from, but it's never that clear. I don't dream about the past. Just about the farm. Being trapped there with ghosts or serial killers or monsters..."

And he'd brought it all to the surface, poking around in the shreds of her past. "You have a chance to reclaim that place now. Turn it into something good instead of what you remember."

She just stared at him. "Do you believe in ghosts?"

He believed in echoes, the kinds that followed people no matter where they went. "I think we can be haunted by things, yes. By the past."

"I always thought the farm was haunted." She rolled to her side and reached for him with her other hand. "The whole pack has so much to be haunted by. I hope there's room in the house for all the new ghosts."

Jay hesitated, then crawled onto the bed and curled up behind her. "There's no ghosts, honey. Just pain, and that fades in time."

Her wolf's power seethed just beneath her skin, wounded and wary, but Eden squirmed back against Jay in silent acceptance of his protection. "You never told me your secrets."

No, he hadn't, and now he found himself more reluctant to do so than ever before. More ghosts, more pain. "When I said I understand what you went through, watching what happened to Zack, it wasn't entirely true. To be honest, I'm more familiar with his side of the whole equation."

She twined their fingers together. "I'm sorry."

"Not your fault." The words came automatically, a reassurance he couldn't help but offer. "I'm glad Zack had your mom and dad, not to mention you. Family who cared."

Eden rolled over and stared up at him. "He made me promise never to tell. Made me swear when I was so young I can't even remember doing it. And he was my hero, my protector. I think I would have told any lie he wanted me to."

All he could give her was the brutal truth, layer one more blanket of cruelty on her world. "You couldn't have stopped what was happening to him, Eden. It isn't as though no one knew. There were investigations, examinations. They figured Albus couldn't be beating Zack because he always healed too fast. They wouldn't have listened to the truth."

"I could have told my parents. If they'd known how bad it was..." She clenched her hand around the blankets. "It's not right that people can *know* and not fix it."

"No," he agreed. "But when you have to hide away, you lose some of the protections people take for granted. Look at what happened in Memphis."

"Zack talked like all the cities are like that. Is it really that bad everywhere?"

"Not in the smaller towns." And not in the sanctuaries.

The import of what they were about to do hit Jay like a punch. As soon as his friends arrived, they'd be making a stand, probably even traveling to Memphis to deliver their message in person. From now on, Clover would be a safe place, a haven where wolves in need could take shelter.

More would come—provided he could hold the line and keep other alphas out of Clover.

Eden pushed up on one elbow and studied him. "You thought of something." She placed her hand on his chest. "Something that made your heart beat faster."

She'd be in for the long haul, even if she had no idea what they were in for, and it was his job to teach her. "Do you know what sanctuary means?"

Her eyebrows drew together. "Only in a human context. Does it mean something special for werewolves?"

"It means everything." He settled his head on the extra pillow and let his hand rest on her hip. "The cities are bad, like Zack said. Most of them have alphas who take what they want and don't really give a damn about anything else. Sanctuaries are different. They're about safety."

After a moment she stretched out to face him, her hand tucked under her chin. "Is that what we're going to do? Turn the farm into some sort of sanctuary?"

"If I don't, the wolves from Memphis will keep coming after Zack and the others."

"Oh." A moment's silence as her gaze roamed over his face. "And they'll respect that? It seems too easy. Why wouldn't everyone do it?"

"They'll respect it because they have to. Because we'll kill them if they don't."

Her breathing hitched, and she squeezed her eyes shut. "I'm still not used to how good that feels to hear."

He wouldn't start any fights, but he damn sure wouldn't sit by and let others get hurt or killed by his inaction. "We'll do what it takes, Eden. I promised you—if your cousin came here in need, we'd help him, right?"

"You did." When she opened her eyes again, the blue was lost to glowing gold. "Do you know what scares me most?"

Likely an intangible, something he couldn't wrestle into submission with his bare hands. "Tell me."

"I want to hurt them." The words were barely a whisper, a rasped confession. "All those years of watching helplessly, but now I feel strong. And I want to find the men who harmed Zack and tear out their throats."

A woman like her, who abhorred violence and had never lifted a hand to another in her life—no wonder it confused her. "Protection, Eden, not vengeance. Don't do yourself the disservice of confusing them, okay?"

"It feels the same. It feels...vicious."

Only time would teach her the visceral and very real difference between the impulses twisting her and wanton anger. For now, he pulled her tighter, tucked her face against his neck. "Sleep, and trust me. Just for now."

The tension bled from her body a bit at a time until she was soft and pliable, cuddled up as close as she could be. Her breath tickled his throat as she sighed. "I do, you know. I trust you. Not just for now."

"Good." Trust, first, and then no more words. He'd show her, instead—what it meant to be a wolf, to be alpha.

What it meant to belong to him.

Chapter Five

Jay set the cardboard tray of coffee cups on the rickety table and stepped back. "Thanks for coming in so quickly. I'd say I owe you, but I think we already know that's true from way back."

"We all owe each other," Colin drawled lazily as he claimed a cup. "No one keeps track except Shane, and he can't help himself."

"I keep track of plenty of things," Shane retorted, his fingers still clicking on the keys of his laptop. "But not that." He stopped typing and closed the machine. "You said this had to do with Memphis."

"Memphis." Jay took his own seat in the tiny kitchen. The smaller house on the farm was just that—small—but it was the only place where any privacy could be found, and they needed it for the discussion they were about to have. "Turns out, the rumors are true."

Colin's expression hardened into one of dark fury. "All of them?"

"Near as I can tell. A handful of enforcers got together, overthrew their alpha, and now they're running wild down there. Rape, torture, you name it."

Fletcher cut off Colin's angry snarl with a hand on the other wolf's arm. "If some of their victims are here, you've got to choke it down, Colin. I'd wager they can't handle rage of any sort right now."

"No, far from it." Jay began to pass out the rest of the coffees. "The enforcers targeted a smaller pack in the city. Took their alpha when he wouldn't fall in line—that's Zack. With him out of the way, it was open season. They toyed with the ones that amused them and killed the ones that didn't. So, right now, I have three top priorities. One for each of you. Shane—"

"I know." He gave a small salute. "I'm nice and non-threatening, so I'll be dealing with the refugees."

"You're the only one not likely to scare the shit out of them," Jay agreed. "Colin, I need you to hit your contacts hard and find out everything you can about these assholes in Memphis. We need a game plan."

Colin shook off Fletcher's hand. "Fine," he grated out. "But it better end with us wiping these bastards out of existence."

Fletcher caught Jay's gaze and held it for a moment before deliberately shifting the conversation. "So Colin's making phone calls, and Shane's petting and soothing. What's that leave for me?"

"A different kind of babysitting." The kind that would break Eden's heart if she knew. "Zack. Who the hell knows what those bastards did to him? He's had a few shaky moments—to be expected, I know, but we need to be sure that's the extent of it. I don't think he'd ever forgive me if I let him hurt someone."

"All right, I can do that." He lifted both eyebrows. "Do you need me to start signing checks while I'm at it? This place is looking pretty sparse, Ancheta."

Fletcher could well afford it, but Jay shook his head. "I'll hold you to that when we figure out something long-term. If we're not generating some kind of income, money's a moot point."

"Paying it back's a moot point," Fletcher argued, leaning forward to brace his elbows on the table. "Having it's damn important, whether you're generating income or not. Come on, man. They deserve a few creature comforts."

"And I'm going to handle it. I'll take plenty of your money, Fletch, believe me, but I'll do it later."

"Not even for essentials?" he pressed.

"Maybe," Jay finally allowed. "Drop it?"

Fletcher didn't back down the way Colin or Shane might, but after a moment he nodded, indicating that he was willing to step aside and recognize Jay's place as leader. For now.

"This house is where we're staying?" Colin asked, filling the silence.

"Yeah." Better for everyone if the strong newcomers stayed separate from everyone else—at least for a while. "There's one more thing I've got to say. I don't think I need to, but I'd hate for there to be misunderstandings later."

Fletcher's gaze turned considerably more wary. "And that is?"

"The women," he answered bluntly. "They've been through a lot, and it's sheer instinct for them to look for something solid now. Something safe. But it's a bad idea."

Shane almost choked on a sip of coffee, and Fletcher snorted. It was Colin who eyed him with amused disbelief. "Good advice. Maybe you should take it, since the snarly little blonde smells like she slept under you last night."

Leave it to Colin to call him out on perceived hypocrisy. "The snarly blonde's not from Memphis. Eden is Zack's cousin, and I've known her for years. She was just turned and has no Guide, obviously, so it's up to me."

Colin sat back and ran a hand over his dark hair. "Ah, shit. Well, that explains why she feels so...volatile. Have you thought about getting someone down here to perform an official Guide-Initiate bonding?"

Shane opened his laptop again. "I have a friend who'd do it in a heartbeat."

Jay rose with a nod. "We need Guide magic," he agreed, "not to mention some heavy-duty wards around the farm. Nothing too fancy, but I'm betting they'll take some time."

"You need a pack witch," Fletcher said quietly. "All the safest sanctuaries have them. That *is* what you want to do here, isn't it? Sanctuary?"

It was still hard to say it out loud, to commit to such a monumental undertaking. As a cop, he was responsible for people's safety all the time, every day. But that responsibility ended when potential danger did. They needed him for moments—sometimes the worst of their lives, but moments nonetheless.

He'd never been needed as an alpha.

"Sanctuary," he confirmed. "That's what I'm doing. We'll have to declare it, and that means going to Memphis. Part of me agrees with Colin, you know. Let 'em come here expecting to find Zack and the others...and find us instead. But the rest of me knows it'd be too traumatic. If even one of them got past us—" He shuddered. It was exactly what had happened to Eden. "It's too risky."

Colin hesitated for a moment before nodding. Fletcher grinned and lifted his coffee. "A sanctuary right on top of a human town. You've got big brass balls, my friend."

Jay snorted. "Why do you think we need those wards so damn bad? Find me a witch, Shane."

"Done." He grinned over the top of the monitor. "Stella has to make arrangements and check with her alpha, but she's going to get back to me by the end of the day."

"Stella..." Colin narrowed his eyes. "She's the one apprenticed to Keith Winston's witch, isn't she? Up in Red Rock?"

"That's her. She was mentioning just the other day that it's time for her to do some work on her own."

"Then we'll be glad to have her." Jay arched an eyebrow. "Fletcher will even pay her, since he's hot to start writing checks."

Fletcher grinned. "My signing fingers are tingling already. I've always wanted to buy a witch."

"Hire a witch," Shane corrected. "You talk like that around Stella and she'll bite your signing fingers off."

"Good. She'll fit right in with Jay's snarly blonde." Fletcher met Jay's eyes, and there was a hint of challenge there. A lazy demand that Jay step up to the line. "She *is* yours, right?"

Eden was exactly the sort of woman Fletcher couldn't resist. Jay suppressed a growl. "Yeah, she's mine."

"Well, then. Best to avoid temptation altogether. All the ladies are off limits." Fletcher punched Colin on the shoulder lightly. "You hear that?"

Colin growled. "You touch me one more time, you're going to lose that hand."

"Jesus, Colin. I hope you're more charming with the ladies."

"I don't *need* to be charming with the ladies. My face isn't half as busted as yours."

Jay pinched the bridge of his nose. "We'll go to Memphis tomorrow. Shane can stay here and look out for the place. In the meantime...try not to kill each other?"

Colin stood and jerked his head toward Shane. "You need help unpacking your gear?"

"I brought my bike, so there's not much." Shane swept up his computer as he rose from the table. "Have to get my wireless signal booster set up, though, if you're looking for something to do."

"Sounds like a party."

Fletcher lingered as the two men stomped down the porch steps. "You've got your hands full, all right."

"Yeah." He squinted at his oldest friend. "What was that? That look you gave me about Colin?"

Sighing, Fletcher rubbed a hand over his face. "It's getting to him. He ignored me when I told him to take it slow with the vigilante work. That shit'll eat you up if you let it, and he's been hip deep in it for a few years now without stopping to breathe."

And Jay was dragging him to Memphis, possibly for more bloodshed. "If we can get past the immediate danger, maybe he'll agree to stick around for a while. Take it easy."

"I think he needs to." The look in Fletcher's eyes was deadly serious. "He's been calling me more than he used to, and lately it hasn't just been as a friend. He needs an alpha. Ask him to stay, and I'm pretty sure he will. Maybe for a long time."

Colin wasn't like Fletcher. With a good enough reason—for a good enough leader—Colin would sublimate his own alpha tendencies and content himself with helping to run a pack. Fletcher, on the other hand, would push and push, driven to challenge because his instincts would accept nothing less.

No, Colin wasn't like Fletcher, who'd never stay. Who would wander until he formed or took on a pack of his own.

"He might stay," Jay agreed. "I know you won't. I get that too."

"I'll stay until everything's settled," Fletcher promised. "I want to help you, because I can believe in this. But once we're out of enemies to fight together, you know what'll happen."

The squabbling would start—not petty, silly shit, but actual arguments arising from the fundamental differences in the way they approached problems. "I can take it. Can you?"

"Of course we can take it." He glanced at the door. "It's unfair to the rest of them, though. There can only be one leader. I'll follow as long as I can and leave when I can't."

"Who knows? You might find something worth sticking around for."

"Because *that* worked out well for me last time around."

Rebecca. To say that Fletcher's last serious entanglement had ended in disaster was an unqualified understatement. "Shit. I'm sorry, man. I didn't mean to bring that up."

"It's forgotten." Fletcher rose with his coffee cup in hand. "Do you want me to get right on the babysitting, or do you mind if I borrow your girl for a couple hours and write my first check?" He nodded toward the empty fridge on the other side of the kitchen. "We need a whole lot of food if we're setting up camp. Might as well stock everyone's pantries."

Jay's first instinct was to deny him the time alone with Eden. His second was to smile. "You'll have to ask her."

"Smart man."

By the time she started her third batch of biscuits, Eden was starting to feel almost accomplished. The slight singe around the edges of the first batch hadn't stopped hungry werewolves from devouring them in minutes.

She used her grandmother's measuring cups to dump enough flour for a double batch into the large ceramic bowl and smiled ruefully at Lorelei. "You weren't joking. A house full of werewolves can eat a *lot.*"

The other woman smiled a little. "No, I wasn't joking."

Such a tiny smile, but Eden was learning to count each one as a step forward. "Well, my father's finally going to get his wish. I'm learning the family business."

"Does he want you to take over the diner someday?"

"I don't think he cares about the diner as much as just being able to leave me something." Eden twirled her hand, her gesture taking in the farmhouse. "This was his legacy, before everything went wrong. The diner belonged to my mother's family."

Lorelei dusted flour over the butcher's block. "Zack never mentioned this place. I didn't know it existed until he started talking about bringing everyone here."

"I'm not surprised. Growing up was tough, and Zack's father..." Eden glanced at Lorelei, unsure how much Zack had shared and unwilling to tread on what little privacy her cousin had left. "No one was really happy here."

"It's a shame." Lorelei wiped her hands on a kitchen towel, her expression sympathetic but also somehow matter-of-fact. "Is that dough ready?"

"Just about." Eden turned toward the fridge to retrieve the buttermilk and froze when a glance out the front window showed Mrs. Wilson lugging an oversized basket up the driveway. "Oh, hell. We're about to have company."

Lorelei froze. "It's not—" Her voice cracked, and she shook her head. "Who?"

"No," Eden said quickly, cursing her verbal clumsiness. "No, it's just the neighbor from the farm down the road. She's harmless, but she's nosy. She's the one who called Jay when you guys first showed up."

"What could she possibly want?"

Eden wiped off her hands with a wry smile. "You're not from a small town, are you?"

Lorelei groaned. "A bunch of women living here with your hoodlum cousin. That's what this is about."

Judging by the size of the basket, Mrs. Wilson had been counting the number of people who came in and out of the farm. "We were always going to have to deal with this eventually. How good are you at charming old ladies?"

"Honestly? I suck at charming anyone who isn't trying to get in my pants."

"Oh boy." Eden eyed Lorelei for a moment and couldn't help her grin. "I guess I could always pass you off as my cousin. You look more like me than Zack does."

Lorelei nodded. "Let's go with it."

"Dad's side of the family," Eden decided, throwing the towel over her shoulder as Mrs. Wilson's footsteps creaked up the porch steps. "We'll just say family's reclaiming the farm and leave it at that for now."

"Got it."

Mrs. Wilson knocked, and Eden counted silently to five before crossing to the door to pull it open with a smile. "Mrs. Wilson, how nice to see you."

"Pleasure's mine, Eden." She held up the basket, her gaze already sliding past Eden and over the interior of the house. "Is this a bad time?"

If she didn't let the woman in, Mrs. Wilson would only be more convinced that something deviant and illicit was happening behind the closed doors of the farm. Lifting the basket from the old woman's hands, Eden stepped back and nodded toward the open archway to the kitchen. "My cousin and I were just making biscuits, but if you'd like to come in and have some tea, you can meet her."

Her eyes lit on Lorelei. "Your cousin?"

Lorelei smiled and held out her hand. "How do you do?"

"Mrs. Wilson, this is Lorelei. She's my second cousin once removed, maybe? Or third cousin." Eden faked a lighthearted laugh as Lorelei shook hands. "I can never remember how those work. Anyway, she's come to help us turn the farm around. I'm sorry I forgot to call and warn you that they were on their way in. Chief Ancheta told me you were keeping an eye on the place, and I appreciate it so much."

"Of course," the old woman murmured. "They?"

"Yes, a few of the cousins and some of their friends." Eden pulled out a chair with a bright smile. "Sit, sit. Lorelei, could you get some of the sweet tea from the fridge?"

Lorelei flashed her a look behind Mrs. Wilson's back. "I'd love to."

Eden bit the inside of her cheek until she was sure she wasn't going to smile in response. She would not laugh. She would *not* laugh. "How have you been, Mrs. Wilson? Well, I hope? Any visits from your grandchildren lately?"

"Oh no, dear. Not since last month. They're back in school now, you know."

"Of course, how silly of me." She held the kitchen chair until the old woman had lowered herself into it, then took the seat next to her. "I hope we haven't been too loud for you, with the renovations." There. An opening for the woman to voice her complaints. The quicker she got around to it, the quicker Eden could hustle her on back out the door.

"Mostly the coyotes, dear. They've been terribly noisy, but that situation should rectify itself once deer season starts."

Mrs. Wilson had to be mistaking the wolf howls for coyotes. Lord, would the hunters make the same mistake? Surely Jay must know enough to be careful, if he'd been running around Clover all this time without getting shot.

Presumably. Hell, maybe he *had* been shot, and she just didn't know. It was one more worry to add to the list. "Of course," she said faintly. "Well, we should be finished fixing up both houses soon, in any case."

"Both?" The woman raised an eyebrow. "How many of your cousins have come to stay here?"

Eden ground her teeth together through a smile. "Just a few, but there will be workers too. Putting the farm to rights will take a lot of hard work."

Lorelei delivered the glasses of tea, and Mrs. Wilson smiled at her. "Are y'all going to grow soybeans like everyone else? I swear, no one does any of the specialty crops anymore. No place to sell them."

"We're still debating some of the particulars," Eden hedged when Lorelei said nothing. "Concentrating on the barn and fixing the place up. We're going to get a few animals, and one of the girls has a very nice business. Lorelei, why don't you go and see if Mae has a gift box we could give to Mrs. Wilson?"

"Okay." Lorelei shot out of the kitchen, leaving Eden alone with the puzzled-looking Mrs. Wilson.

The woman sipped her tea before speaking. "I thought you meant they were helping you get your farm going, Eden, but it sounds as though everyone's staying."

Eden met the implied question with a bland smile. "Not *everyone*, but it's not just my farm, you know. And I still have a job in town, so I can't be here to manage things." Odd, that those words already made her feel vaguely hollow. There would be a time when she couldn't be here every day to help, and it felt...wrong.

"Oh." Mrs. Wilson toyed with the lemon wedge on the rim of her glass. "I thought the farm *was* just yours. I assumed, you know, when Albus died and Zachary didn't come home for the funeral."

On paper, it *did* belong to her. Albus's last defiant gesture, leaving everything he owned to Eden. As much as she'd wanted her father to reconcile with his brother for his own peace of mind, Eden was fervently glad Zack hadn't returned for his father's final, bitter days. Albus's body might have failed, but his mind and his vicious hatred had stayed as sharp as ever.

"We're family," she told Mrs. Wilson, just like she'd told her father. Just like she'd tell Zack. "I may own the farm, but it belongs to all of the Greens. That's how it should be, don't you think?"

"But will Zachary ever come back to it?"

The old biddy hadn't seen him yet. Eden considered lying, but Zack's presence would come out eventually, and everything she'd ever said on the topic would be scrutinized by Mrs. Wilson and everyone she knew. "He's already here. Working hard on the barn right now, I think."

The woman straightened, obviously taken aback. "I didn't know that."

Lorelei hadn't returned. Eden was starting to envy her. "Yes, he's been here for a few days. He came with Lorelei and the others."

"I see."

Silence stretched out, expanding and growing until it was a tangible presence every bit as real as Mrs. Wilson, who stared at her in awkward discomfort, clearly at a loss for words.

Well, words she'd say to Zack's cousin, in any case.

Eden cleared her throat and gestured to the barely touched glass. "Can I get you some more sweet tea?"

A good deal of the older woman's indulgent courtesy had chilled. "Actually, I should be going. You will keep the construction noise down, won't you, Eden?"

You hadn't even heard it until you found out Zack was here. This was how it would be from now on. Zack didn't have to do anything to be guilty. If the town couldn't find a crime he'd committed, they'd make one up.

They always had.

It was hard to smile when she wanted to bare her teeth in a snarl, but Eden managed. She smiled until her jaw ached. "Of course, Mrs. Wilson. Thanks so much for the basket."

"You're welcome, honey." The woman rose and returned Eden's smile. "And tell your daddy I asked after him, all right?"

"Absolutely. Let me walk you out."

She kept her smile fixed in place like it'd been stapled there until the door was shut with her adversary on the other side. The wolf stirring inside her wouldn't view the old woman as anything else, not when Mrs. Wilson invaded their territory and stank up the room with disapproval and chilly disdain.

Too bad for Mrs. Wilson, and too bad for every nosy gossip in Clover. Eden wasn't a helpless kid this time around, and no one was going to drive Zack away from his home.

Lorelei peeked around the open archway into the living room. "I hid. I'm not proud of that fact, but there it is."

Eden laughed hoarsely and closed her eyes. "That just makes you smart."

"I heard bits and pieces. She thinks we're starting a filthy hippie commune and that Zack's the Antichrist."

"They've always thought that, ever since he was a teenager." Eden pushed away from the door and headed back for the kitchen island. "It's not going to get better once they see him. The tattoos are a bit much for Clover."

Lorelei lingered, staring at the front door with a troubled expression. "We'll have to be careful, won't we?"

It had always been the truth, but maybe the wolves who were used to the city hadn't understood. "People around here think they have a right to know everything about everyone. And when we start selling soap and lotion and handspun fabric..."

Hippie commune, indeed.

Chapter Six

Jay felt Zack's approach in the jagged, discordant power that flowed ahead of him, but Eden's cousin didn't say a word until he'd dropped a cardboard package of beer down hard enough to rattle the glass bottles within. "Thought you might be thirsty."

Jay finished hammering in the nail he'd placed to secure the barn window casement. "Thanks. I could use one."

Zack claimed one bottle and sat in one of the folding chairs situated among the building supplies. "Fair warning. It's a bribe."

Interesting. Jay eyed him as he dropped to the other chair. "What do you need?"

"That wolf who's following me around."

Fletcher couldn't have already made an ass of himself, but maybe Zack was looking for confirmation more than anything else. "I asked him to keep an eye on you," Jay confessed.

Zack stared at empty air and took a slow sip of his beer. "So he doesn't want to be my new best friend."

"You sound relieved."

"Don't really want a new best friend." Another sip. "Mine hasn't been dead all that long."

Lorelei had explained—in hushed, sad tones—about Zack's roommate, Noah, and his attempts to hold the pack together after Zack's abduction and supposed death. "I'm sorry."

Zack shrugged, his gaze still fixed on that empty bit of space, but not like he was staring forward, unseeing. He could have been looking at something—or someone. "I lost a lot more than just Noah. I'd be watching me like a hawk too."

Chilling words, nearly the last ones Jay wanted to hear. "You seem to be doing okay, all things considered."

"All things considered. Maybe I'm still trying to wrap my head around it. Never thought I'd end up back here."

"Can't say as I blame you." The farm was beautiful, but it wasn't peaceful. It wasn't settled. "You'll get past it. You've got a lot of good things going."

"I do, do I?"

"Sure. Everyone's relatively safe here, and you've got Eden and Austin looking out for you."

Zack's mouth twitched toward a smile. "Eden looking out for me. God, that makes me feel *old.*"

"Not the kid you remember, huh?" Jay sobered. "I would have talked to you about Fletcher first, but I wasn't sure how you'd take it. Alpha to alpha, I mean."

The smile fell away, leaving Zack's gaunt face blankly exhausted. "If there's anything alpha left in me, it's needing to keep them safe. Lorelei, Mae, Quinn...Kaley. They're the important ones."

And yet he'd been the glue holding them all together. Jay shook his head. "You don't really think it's that simple, do you?"

"It has to be, for now. I haven't got a damn thing left to give."

Oh, but there was plenty his pack still wanted from him— one young alpha in particular. "You think Kaley's going to want to accept that? Or understand it, even if she does?"

That snared the full force of Zack's attention. Dark eyebrows pulled together over narrowed eyes, and Zack's power bubbled up. "Kaley's young, and still fairly new. She'll learn, and she'll move on."

The words carried a thread of desperation, but Jay only nodded. "Maybe."

"She *will.*"

"I heard you."

"Aren't exactly acting like you believe me."

"Because I don't," Jay answered. "I'm not real well acquainted with Kaley, not yet, but she doesn't seem like the type to let stuff go. Not if it's important to her."

Zack ground his teeth together audibly. "I'm the only wolf she's ever known who's stronger than her. That'd confuse anyone who's new."

There was hope for the man yet, if he could come to his alpha with his tail tucked between his legs and still manage to get in a dig about Eden. "I'm not railroading your cousin, Zack."

"Better not be." Zack's smile returned, and this time it held a vicious edge. "Can't say I wasn't wondering if that was part of the reason you sent Fletcher after me. Get him out of the way and all."

"I'm not that manipulative." Jay sipped his beer. "*Or* insecure."

"Good for you." After a moment, Zack shrugged. "I don't care if he babysits me. As long as he'll help with the repairs."

"Fletch isn't afraid to get his hands dirty."

"And if I snap? He'll do the dirty work there too?"

An almost hopeful question—completely out of place, considering what he was asking. "You want to know if Fletcher would kill you?"

Zack finished his beer and reached for a second one. "Someone better be willing to, if the worst happens. You wouldn't have him watching me if you didn't know that."

"Information," Jay countered. "Got to know if someone's headed off the rails."

"And when they're already there?" Scowling, Zack twisted the cap off his beer and flung it aside. "I don't need a fucking pep talk. I need to know you've got the balls to do what it takes to keep my people safe."

Eden would hate him, not to mention the rest of Zack's pack. "I'll do what I have to do." It was the closest Jay could come to a promise, and it was true. If there was no other way, no hope left... "But *I* will do it. I won't have anyone else handle my shit work. And if you think me saying this is a free pass to give up, think again, pal."

Zack bared his teeth in a grin that stopped a hairsbreadth short of outright challenge. "Can't give up, can I? It's not over yet."

"Not even close." Jay snagged another beer. "But it won't be over when we beat Memphis back, either. That's just the start."

"Not really looking that far ahead right now. One foot in front of the other...unless I fall off the path." Zack stared at Jay. "Don't let me hurt them. Swear to me."

"I swear."

But the whole conversation left him on edge, disquieted. Not because of what Zack was saying, but because of the unspoken implications. The feeling Jay couldn't shake that, no matter what he said, the other wolf just needed to know he could slip away, guilt-free.

Jay's couch was starting to feel more like home than any place in her own house ever had.

It was the smell, Eden decided as she settled next to her. His scent had become the one thing she associated with safety. The tense muscles of her neck began to relax as she inhaled deeply and let her wolf rise to the surface. Not enough to spill free, but enough to loosen her limbs as she twisted to rub her cheek against his shoulder. "This is what gets me through the day. This moment right here."

"Good." He slipped his arm around her shoulders. "Did you and Fletch buy out the grocery store?"

"Just about. And the fabric store, and the hardware store." She smiled. "Is he secretly a prince?"

"More like very well-managed, very *old* money."

"Well, he was very generous in spending it." Closing her eyes, Eden traced her fingers over Jay's chest. "Mae smiled for the first time when she saw the sewing machine we brought home. Did you know she's an artist? She does a lot of different things, but one of her specialties is textiles. I guess that was part of her and Kaley's plan. The reason they were coming to the farm to begin with."

He hummed softly. "I thought it was Zack's idea to come to the farm."

"It was Zack's idea to come to *this* farm. Kaley told me that she and Mae had been making plans for a while. Mae has a pretty decent business selling soaps and lotions, but she also makes hand-spun, hand-dyed yarn, and they thought they could expand by raising and shearing their own animals."

Jay sat up a little straighter and squinted down at her. "What, you mean like sheep?"

She bit back a grin. "Alpacas, actually. Apparently there can be good money there, if you know how to raise animals and how to sell the fiber."

"Who knows how to raise them?"

"Kaley. She's familiar with the requirements." Jay had a furrow between his eyebrows, and she couldn't resist the urge to smooth it away, stroking her finger down the bridge of his nose with a smile. "I know it sounds pretty out there, but they've given it a lot of thought. They have money set aside, and supplies squirreled away in a storage unit outside of Memphis.

That's one of the things they wanted me to ask—if you and the men could clear it out and bring everything back. They didn't have time after Zack escaped."

Jay nodded his agreement. "If we can, we'll get it."

"I understand." A shiver of foreboding swept over her, and she pressed her forehead to his cheek and tried to banish the sudden chill with the warmth of his body. "I hate that you have to go at all."

He held her closer and spoke low against her ear. "The only other option is to let them come here."

Yes, the wolf whispered deep inside her. Let the enemies come to them. Let her fight as an alpha should. Let her defend her pack.

Only her pack had enough scars already, and she had no experience with fighting. She swallowed the urge and nodded. "I know. I still hate it, but I understand."

He stroked her hair. "I asked Shane about your early change. He said he's never heard of anything like that happening without magical interference, but he's going to do some research."

Shane's computer had proven to be a treasure trove of supernatural lore and ancient texts, each book lovingly scanned and catalogued with a thoroughness that had piqued her curiosity and earned her professional respect. If an explanation for her current situation couldn't be found in the endless pages of information he'd amassed...

Unease crawled over her skin. She focused on Jay's fingers in her hair and on taking slow, steady breaths. "My vacation and personal days will take me through the full moon, but after that I have to go back to work or lose my job. Do you think I'll be steady enough by then?"

"It's a very good possibility, though there is another one."

Judging by the tightness in her chest, she'd need it. "What is it?"

"It's old magic, something the witch Shane contacted will be able to do." He stroked her hair again, the touch followed this time by a wave of soothing power. "A Guide bond, a connection between a new wolf and a mentor, of sorts. It can help balance you until you get back on your feet."

A bond. She already felt like she had one with him, a connection that made every touch sizzle or soothe far more than it should. How much more intense would such a thing be with magic? Or maybe helping her process the overwhelming sensory input was the point. "How does it work?"

"It links us together so that I absorb all the excess power that causes you problems. I can do it already, but the bond makes it effortless."

She heard the words, and heard the meaning under them. *Us. I.* "You want to be my Guide?"

He blinked, as if the question startled him. "Yeah, I do. I mean, your choices are limited anyway because of your strength. But...yes."

Eden smoothed her thumb over his lower lip with a self-conscious smile. "And it won't be complicated by how much time I spend wanting to kiss you?"

He cleared his throat and adopted a serious expression, though the way his lips kept curving up at the corners ruined it. "Actually, it's not uncommon for the relationship to include a sexual component."

"Really now?" It wasn't the wolf who prodded her to slide into his lap. She straddled his thighs and rested her hands on his shoulders, fighting to keep her own expression deadly serious. "Jay Ancheta, are you trying to lure me into some kinky sex magic?"

He held up both hands. "Hey, I said you had limited choices, not none. There's Fletcher, Colin, even Shane." The words were easy, but a thread of tension ran through them.

Her wolf surged to the surface, demanding to exploit his unexpected weakness. Make him jealous, make him fight for the right to possess. Eden slapped her down hard enough to make them both reel from the internal battle before framing Jay's face with her hands.

"You're already my guide to werewolf things in all the ways that matter," she whispered. "If it'll make it easier, I want to be bound to you. Kinky sex magic would be a bonus, as long as *you* want to go there with *me*. Because I'm mostly trying to keep from ripping your clothes off right now."

He rasped her name and wrapped his hands around her waist. "Sex is too dangerous right now. You don't have the control for it, not yet. You haven't even faced your first full moon."

"No sex?" His hands were strong. Even his innocent grip felt dirty, felt more like challenge and invitation than caution. "That's not fair."

His fingers slipped under her shirt to stroke her back. "It's not?"

"No." Just one little rock to align her hips over his, and she wanted to groan in relief when she ground down against his erection. Arousal accompanied so many of his touches that it had become like background static, an embarrassing state of almost-turned-on that flamed into need when his skin brushed hers.

She could come like this. It wouldn't take much. A little grind, riding him *and* the thrill of holding the dominant position while the strength of his fingers warned her he could take it away at any moment.

She wanted him to try.

He growled and scratched his nails down her spine. "Eden..."

Too gentle. She bared her teeth and grabbed his shirt, winding her fingers in the fabric before jerking. It ripped with a satisfying noise, revealing his beautiful, glorious chest.

He caught her mouth in a rush of teeth and tongue, a kiss that pleasured as much as it controlled. His fingers dropped to her hips, tightened and rocked her harder against his body. His teeth scraped her lips, dug in. Dominance. It was in every line of him, every movement, in the way he'd taken control of her.

It made her hot. Hungry. Power rose inside her, meeting dominance with strength, with challenge. She tore her mouth from his and tilted her head back, panting for breath. "Is this us not having sex?"

He released a shaky sigh. "Much more and your wolf's going to want out. It's nothing to play around with, Eden. It hurts."

out out out

Eden pressed both hands to her chest as the wolf surged to the surface, like the beast could fly out of their human skin. "Can I change when it's not the full moon? Can I choose to change?"

"Yes," he whispered against her throat. "But you have to make sure it's you choosing to do it, not her fighting her way out."

"Oh, she's fighting. Seems like she always is." Eden closed her eyes and tried to quiet her body, but it was too late to dial back arousal. Jay's breath skidding over her throat sent shocking tingles straight to her core. "The first night, you did something. You bit the back of my neck and she stopped fighting."

"It wasn't the bite." Jay brushed his lips over the hollow of her throat, and the tingles spread, solidified into a feeling of well-being, of *rightness*. It felt like dropping into a soft chair after a long day, like slipping between cool sheets at night, every knot in her body unraveling as her toes curled. She moaned, wallowed in it.

Jay's low growl subsided into a pleased rumble. "See? Once we're bound together, that's all the time. That easy."

Eden dropped her face to hide in the crook of his neck and let her body relax against his. "Soon?"

"As soon as this mess with Memphis is done."

A few days, at most. Eden listened to the strong, swift beat of his heart and let go of the last of her anticipation. Sex could wait. Probably *should* wait, considering how much of it seemed tied up in a feral sort of insanity.

They could be something more than urges. "Jay?"

"Hmm?"

She didn't know the words for what she wanted to say. She wasn't sure they existed. "They're ours, aren't they? The pack? They feel like mine. *You* feel like mine."

His chest shook under her cheek, a soft chuckle that washed over her, warm and sweet. "Ours. We'll take care of them, honey. I promise."

Chapter Seven

Eden tucked the fitted sheet under the foot of the new mattress and slid her hand over the soft cotton with a smile. "There you go, Quinn. Better than a sleeping bag, I hope."

He offered her a faint smile. "I'm used to roughing it. The bag would have been fine."

"Well, the bed will be better." Straightening, she propped her hands on her hips and eyed the rest of the room. Though the farmhouse had been a warren of sad, empty bedrooms for as long as Eden could remember, the rooms stood testament to a time when the Greens and their extended family had filled the halls with love and laughter.

Now they were filling again, as quickly as Eden could clean them. Quinn was the quietest of the wolves who'd arrived with Zack. The bruised look in his eyes and the careful way he moved made Eden all the more determined to give him a little bit of something he could call his own.

Moving to the sliding door, Eden pushed it open, revealing the second story porch. "We can get you a screen door for this if you want. Keep the bugs out but let you enjoy the fresh air."

"That'd be nice," he answered vaguely. "Any more bed frames you need me to assemble?"

Now wasn't the time to push, no matter how much his pain made her ache. "There's one in the bedroom across from Zack's. I thought we could set it up so it will be ready when the witch from Red Rock arrives."

He nodded and left, heading into the large, all-purpose room at the head of the stairs where Mae sat with her sewing machine. Shane knelt by a baseboard, running cable for the internet, though he looked up when Eden walked by. "Let me know if you need any help."

Eden let Quinn go and leaned against the wall to watch Shane. "I think everything's well in hand. I'm just a hovering mama annoying everyone."

He taped down a length of cable and rose. "I think everyone could use it, at least for a while."

"Maybe." And maybe she wasn't the right kind of soothing, not with her own wolf so volatile. "How's the wiring coming? Will we be able to get a decent wireless signal, you think?"

He grinned. "I'm putting a second router up here, Eden. That's what the wires are for. Signal on the one downstairs will never reach, so you're going to have two."

"Whatever works," Eden said, glancing at Mae. The girl had her attention fixed on her sewing like Shane wasn't there, but Eden had watched the tension ease from her in the hour since he'd come upstairs.

Eden had been worried at first when Jay had insisted Shane stay at the farm while the rest of the men went to Memphis, but something about him soothed even the most traumatized wolves. He spoke in murmurs, moved with calculated deliberation and never approached anyone or stood close enough to back them into a corner.

It seemed very, very precise to her—and utterly natural to him.

He met her gaze and stilled. "What?" he asked curiously.

Before she could answer, Kaley stuck her head through the open doorway. "Have any of you guys seen Zack?"

"They're not back yet," Eden said, and Mae whipped around, wide-eyed and pale.

Oh shit.

Kaley stared at Eden, her brown eyes huge in her suddenly pale face. "Back? From Memphis?" She whirled on Mae, her heart pounding loud in the quiet of the room. "He went?"

Mae cringed, shrinking in on herself as if the words had ridden rage instead of terror. Eden stepped between the girls and tried to project confidence along with her words. "He'll be fine, Kaley. Jay and the others are with him."

"No, you don't understand." Kaley's hands shook, and she clenched them into fists. "We're all here. There's no one there he has to protect. That's what Zack wanted, *all* he wanted."

Wild power swept through the room. Strong. Fierce. Mae's chair tipped over with a clatter, but Eden couldn't worry about the girl when her own magic was rising fast and vicious. *Dominate*, it urged, begged, screamed. Kaley's power was a challenge. A rebellion.

Shane stepped forward as Kaley's chest began to rise and fall with harsh, rapid breaths. "Come on, calm down—"

"No." She brushed past him, advancing on Eden. "Don't tell me you haven't seen it, because I know you have. Now that we're all here, he's just waiting to check out. He's—he's—" The words broke on a sound too splintered for a sob, and she bent double with a cry of pain.

Eden gave up thinking and acted on instinct, grabbing Kaley by the shoulders and dragging them both to the floor. "Shh," she whispered, pulling the girl into her lap. Heat spilled from her hands, and she smoothed one up to the back of Kaley's head, unsure what she was doing but driven by something beyond herself. "It's okay. It's all going to be okay."

Kaley shuddered. "He was dead," she babbled. "He was dead and now he's not, but he doesn't believe it."

"We'll make him believe it. We'll have time." She tightened her grip on Kaley and poured all her belief, all her hope into every word. "You're not alone with this anymore. You don't have to be the alpha. Jay's here, and his friends, and me too. We're going to make it better."

Another shudder, and the girl's near-sobs subsided into whimpers. "I'm so tired."

Oh God, Eden's heart ached. She tucked Kaley's face against her shoulder and whispered more words, soothing lies of comfort wrapped in brazen confidence. She poured all of her hope into Kaley and prayed things were going well in Memphis.

If Zack didn't come home, Kaley would be the next to break. But she wouldn't be the last.

Jay cut the engine and peered out at the sprawling, two-story apartment complex. Paint curled off pitted siding, windows had been taped, and at least one door had been broken in recently, the jamb still splintered. "You sure they'll come?"

Zack stared blankly at the broken door. "They'll come."

"Do you want to go inside?"

"Probably should." He rubbed the back of his neck. "Might be some stuff I left behind that no one's picked over yet."

"Eden said people had to leave their things behind." Jay tugged the keys from the ignition. "What happened that last night? Before you went to the farm."

"They were coming to kill everyone." Zack bit off a harsh laugh. "Mostly. The bastard stalking Mae tipped their hand. He didn't want her to get caught up in the purge by mistake, so he showed up and told her to pack her bags like a good girl."

The man had been obsessed enough to follow her. No way would he have risked her getting hurt in the crossfire. "How did you get everyone away?"

"Lorelei." Zack's lips twitched. "She's not the strongest wolf, but she's the one you want around in a crisis. I never had another alpha to help me run the pack, but everyone trusts Lorelei. She kept them calm enough to grab what they could, and Quinn—the blond wolf—he'd gotten us a couple of junky cars none of the Memphis pack would recognize. We were gone before Scott realized Mae had given him the slip. We didn't realize he was fucking crazed enough to pay a witch for a tracking spell."

Fletcher's car pulled up beside the truck, and Jay nodded to him and Colin. "Remember the plan, Zack. We don't fight if we don't have to. Not right now."

"Yeah." Zack reached through the open window to let himself out of the truck, his gaze still fixed on the apartment. "Mae said her friend packed up a U-Haul with all the crap she and Kaley hid in their storage unit. I gotta get that stuff back to her. Them."

Jay followed him. "It goes beyond that. If we start fighting, we can't stop until the leaders of this little revolution are dead, gone. You wouldn't think having a power void could be worse than something like this, but it can. I've seen it happen."

Zack stared at him for a tense moment before turning for the broken door. "I've only got so much in me, Ancheta. You'll have to worry about the world."

"It's not a suggestion, Green. It's an order."

A flinch. "Yes, sir."

Jay hated like hell to press the issue, to get controlling, but if he didn't bring Zack to heel... "You asked me to take care of them the best way I know how. This is it."

"I got it," Zack snapped, a hint of growl hiding under the words. "I don't even want to fight. Do you understand? That's how fucking tired I am. I want to get the girls the shit they need and be gone."

He smashed through the unrepaired door and slammed it behind him. As Jay stood there, chilled by the words, Fletcher moved to stand at his side. "That is one broken-ass wolf, buddy."

Gone. "Zack is Eden's cousin. He can't *be* broken, for her sake if nothing else."

"He's halfway to dead, and his pack knows it." Fletcher crossed his arms over his chest and leaned against the truck. "I was with him when the pink-haired girl showed up to tell him about the U-Haul. She's a clever little thing, made it crystal clear to him that the stuff they'd put aside could give them a real start on the farm. Made something clear to me too."

"What's that?"

"The only thing keeping that man going is the young alpha's safety. Mae must have used Kaley's name a round dozen times. I don't know if she's the carrot or the stick, but she sure does get Zack moving."

"I know." And it was a valuable piece of information. "But I'm not about to dangle her in front of him unless lives are at stake. An alpha doesn't manipulate, right?"

"An alpha shouldn't have to." Fletcher rubbed a hand over his arm with a sigh. "A submissive shouldn't have to, either. It hurts, watching them twist themselves in knots to try to steal the protection they're owed. But I guess Zack's girls are going to need some time before they're ready to come to you. Maybe once this is over."

He sure the hell hoped so. "Colin knows he's not supposed to start shit in there, but keep an eye on him, huh?"

Fletcher glanced back toward his car, where Colin was in the passenger seat, staring at his phone. "We had a chat. I don't think he'll start anything, but if they do..." Fletcher huffed out a breath. "Oh, they'll fucking well regret it. He's in a mood."

Jay walked toward the apartment and gestured for Fletcher to join him. "Did he uncover something else?"

"Yeah. A pair of the enforcers were new to Memphis. Their last alpha ran them out of New York because they were endangering the pack with their sadistic games. Not that the New York alpha objected to the sadism, but they didn't always bother to finish their kills. Human law enforcement found a few victims."

"Franz and Jonas," Zack said, appearing at the doorway, his gaze utterly dead. "They like their women to bleed out under them. Even in Memphis, no one would let them play with wolves—unless it was an alpha bitch who needed to be put in her place or in a shallow grave."

Jesus Christ. Jay groaned and rubbed his face. "We'll add them to the list of things to take care of once we have things in order in Clover."

Zack bared his teeth in a smile. "Only Jonas. Kaley ripped out Franz's throat."

"Way to go, Kaley," Fletcher muttered as he slipped past Zack. Jay saw his shoulders stiffen. "Shit."

"Yeah." Zack stepped aside so Jay could enter the apartment.

The place had been utterly destroyed. Drawers lay on the floor, pulled free of their housings and smashed apart, their contents scattered. Paper and silver shards of broken DVDs littered the front room, the refrigerator had been tipped over in the kitchen, and curses and threats covered the walls in multiple garish shades of spray paint.

All that paled next to the smell, the unmistakable odor of stale human urine that drifted up from the carpet. The wolves who had trashed the place had wanted to make their disdain for Zack as clear as possible—they'd not only ransacked his belongings, they'd marked his home as theirs.

Disgusted, Jay surveyed the room again, looking for anything salvageable beyond the wanton destruction. "Bastards."

Zack leaned against the open door with a sigh. "Better things than people."

The rumble of an engine outside left Jay clenching his hands into fists. "Is that them?"

A black SUV with tinted windows pulled past the door, and Zack tensed. "That's them," he confirmed as Colin's door slammed outside. "If there's only one SUV, they didn't bring the whole crew. Weren't expecting to need them, I guess."

"Good. They'll be less likely to hassle us." Jay stepped back outside, onto the cracked sidewalk edging the front of the apartment building. This part of Memphis was rough, the kind of place where the neighbors would be watching but wouldn't intervene.

Colin fell into place on his left. Zack moved silently to stand at his right, and Fletcher pulled the battered door shut behind them but stayed at Jay's back. "Remember, Colin—"

"I know," Colin snarled, hooking his thumbs through his belt. "No killing them."

Jay wasn't any happier about it than Colin was, but that was his own dirty little secret. His burden to bear as alpha.

The SUV doors opened in unison. Four wolves spilled into the parking lot and arrayed themselves in a crooked line. A tall redhead with dark eyes and a chilling smile took the one step necessary to stand ahead of the rest. "Zachary Green. You're one stubborn son of a bitch, aren't you?"

Zack stared at him.

"You don't talk to him," Jay said firmly. "You talk to *me*."

The redhead shifted his gaze slowly, then took the time to study Jay from his boots to the top of his head with his lips twisted in a sneer of utter derision. "And who the fuck do you think you are?"

Moment of truth. "Jay Ancheta, alpha of the Clover sanctuary. Part of your pack came to me looking for protection, and I've given it to them."

Mutters. One of the wolves bit off a curse. The leader smiled. "Well, I'm Christian Peters, and I've lived in Memphis long enough to know that the closest sanctuary is down in Alabama. I think you're full of shit."

"That's what your buddy Scott thought, too, when he came looking for Mae." Jay shrugged. "He's dead now. Same thing that's going to happen to anyone else from Memphis who tries to violate my sanctuary."

Christian's smile vanished. "So that's what happened to Scott." He seemed to be picking his words more carefully, but the cunning in his eyes was matched by barely restrained fury. "He never had much sense when it came to the girl. I suppose we all have our weaknesses."

"If that's what you want to call it."

A hulking man butted against Christian's shoulder, his teeth bared. "This is bullshit."

Christian held out his arm, blocking the other man. "Watch it, Jonas. The man declared sanctuary. That makes him very dangerous or very, very stupid."

"I don't give a flying *fuck* what he says. I want the other bitch, the one who killed Franz."

Zack lunged so fast Fletcher's hand closed on the empty space where he'd been standing. Jay snatched at Zack's shirt and grabbed his arm, nearly getting yanked off his feet for his trouble.

Too late. Jonas's eyes narrowed, and a slow smile curled his lips. "Uh-huh. Kaley." He drawled out her name. "Tasted real sweet. Bad manners, but I could beat that out of her."

Unchecked power surged. Zack roared his fury and ripped free, leaving half of his shirt in Jay's grip. Christian smiled and stepped aside, letting Jonas charge past him to meet Zack in the middle of the parking lot in a clash of fists.

"Fuck," Fletcher snarled. "Want me to try to pull him back?"

"No." Jay's own fury burned hot. *Fuck it.* He could let them fight it out, take on the rest of them. Destroy the bastards the way they'd trashed Zack's home and the lives of his pack.

His pack. Jay's now. He remembered Eden's voice, sweet and low, murmuring about protecting them—together.

She deserved better than this. They all did.

Jay gave in to the instinct under the anger, let the power of an alpha rise to eclipse everything else. He moved, rushing forward to grab Jonas by the back of the head. He yanked the cursing, spitting wolf out of Zack's clutches, spun and slammed his head down onto the SUV's shiny hood. *"Enough."*

He dropped the man and turned again. It didn't matter if he slumped to the pavement or charged. Jay had friends, *pack*, who would watch his back and make sure Jonas never reached his mark.

No. Instead, Jay strode toward Christian, stopping mere inches from the other alpha's face. "Do you acknowledge the sanctuary, or do I have to pound every one of your fucking faces in right now?"

The other wolf was strong. Dominant, to be sure—enforcers had to be—but when Jay leaned in, Christian leaned back, a tiny, telling retreat.

A dominant, but not alpha. Not a leader.

Christian stepped back and snapped his fingers before pointing at Jonas. One of the silent wolves at his back dragged the dazed man to his feet and hauled him to the cargo area of the SUV. Christian retreated another step and looked past Jay.

"We'll respect your sanctuary, but you keep that feral bastard on a leash and out of our territory."

Fletcher had twisted Zack's arm behind his back, and power spiked from them both as Fletcher spoke, quiet and firm. Colin stood, stone faced and silent.

"This is the last place we want to be," Jay shot back.

"Fine." The man retreated to the passenger side door. "Be clear of the county by sunset, or the pack will come hunting."

"Uh-huh." Jay knew better. Christian had lost face in front of his pack. Even if he was too much of a coward to come after Jay, he'd never forget the humiliation of not being able to put him in his place in his own territory. And he would never, ever forgive.

A problem for another time. Jay turned his back, dismissing the man as soundly as possible. "Colin?"

Colin stayed silent until the SUV peeled out of the parking lot in a screech of tires, leaving the stink of burnt rubber behind. "None of them are strong enough to take control of the rest, and none are willing to step aside. That's good for us. And bad for us."

Good because a pack without a leader couldn't stand. Bad because a pack without a leader didn't know how to do a goddamn thing but fight.

Jay shook off the sense of foreboding. "You straight, Zack?"

"Yeah." Zack shoved a hand through his disheveled hair, pulling at the too-long strands with a growl. "I should have known they'd sink a verbal knife. They do it whenever they can."

"It's all they've got." Jay rubbed the back of his wrist over his forehead. "Let's get this done and get the hell out of here."

The kitchen porch had always been Eden's favorite. The driveway led to the front porch, but years of hungry farmers and hungrier kids had worn a path straight to the kitchen, one everyone followed these days. Her grandmother's rocking chairs were back in their old place, and Eden found the squeaky rhythm soothing as she rocked slowly and listened to the bugs chirping and the fainter noises of Lorelei overseeing the preparation of dinner.

Shane was nearly silent beside her, his feet planted flat on the porch and his chair still. The companionable silence had been welcome at first, but the nervous flutters in her stomach doubled with each second that ticked past. Instead of admiring the view or enjoying the quiet, she strained her eyes looking for the first hint of headlights, the visible confirmation of Jay and Zack's safety that a phone call from enemy territory couldn't provide.

She needed a distraction. She sipped her tea and cleared her throat. "How long have you and Jay known each other?"

"About ten years, I guess. Could be twelve."

"And all four of you worked together?"

He laughed. "More like we didn't, not worth a damn, anyway. We met down in Houston. There was a big pack there— bigger than you'd expect with one guy in charge. He was old and crotchety as hell, and he ran the place like it all belonged to him. I guess because it did."

She'd already witnessed the tension between Jay and Fletcher. Too many strong personalities would be trouble when only one could lead. "So what did you do? Did you all leave together? Or just all leave?"

"We tried to travel together for a while. Finally, we figured out we do better if we can have our own space." He squinted out into the dying evening light. "Dispersal, that's what they call it. You know anything about wolves?"

"A little." She ran her thumb along the edge of her mug and stared into the darkness. "When I was a kid, I read every book in the library that had anything to do with wolves. I wanted to be like Zack. Growing up, he was my hero."

"And he was born a wolf."

His tone was inquisitive enough to express interest in the answer without demanding it. "He was born a wolf," she confirmed. "His mother was one." She hesitated. "And I guess his father was too, whoever he happened to be. His mother seemed pretty certain it couldn't have been my uncle."

"No, it really couldn't have been, huh?" Shane sat forward and braced his elbows on his knees. "This isn't a pretty life. The few wolves who don't wind up dead or traumatized have other problems. They don't fit in with humans, they have urges and instincts they can't necessarily control..."

"So I'm learning." She glanced at him and raised an eyebrow. "I didn't want the wolf to bite me, if that's what you're getting at."

"It wasn't." He met her gaze. "You and Jay are going to do a good job. You've both got it in you."

It felt nice to have the approval of someone who understood, and even better when it came from one of Jay's closest friends. "Thank you. I hope you're going to stick around for a while and help us."

"I think I might."

The door from the kitchen creaked open and Mae slipped out. "Kaley's still out," she said, her voice no louder than the squeak of Eden's chair. "She hasn't slept much since they first came for Zack."

Shane rose, stripped off his hoodie and held it out to Mae. "It's too chilly for no sleeves."

Eden tensed, but Mae didn't recoil. Her gaze stayed fixed on his hand as she reached out and accepted the offering without touching him. Eden held her breath, afraid to upset the quiet balance of the moment as Mae tugged the sweatshirt over her head. It fell to mid-thigh and enveloped her body, but she seemed to relax as the fabric draped around her, just like Eden had relaxed the first morning when she'd wrapped herself in Jay's shirt and taken comfort from being surrounded by the scent of a strong wolf.

Mae pulled up the hood to cover her hair and stared at some point slightly beneath Shane's chin. "Thank you."

"You're welcome."

Eden gestured to the empty rocking chair on her right. "Want to sit with us for a little bit?" *No pressure, no expectations.* The invitation hung between them for a dozen hopeful eternities before Mae nodded and slipped past her to the rocking chair.

Such a tiny bit of trust, but Eden had to fight back a triumphant smile. When Jay was safely home, she'd celebrate this step forward with him.

If he got safely home.

No. When. Eden refused herself the satisfaction of checking her watch as she willed the headlights to appear. She found herself talking to fill up the empty air. "I think we'll have everyone settled in here before the fall festival in town. Y'all are going to love it. There's dancing and a carnival and so much food."

Shane leaned one shoulder against a porch column. "That part sounds good, anyway. Can we bypass social niceties and head straight for the chow?"

Social niceties didn't seem to be Shane's specialty, not when they involved words instead of body language or wolfish instincts. Eden grinned at him. "What if the town girls chase you for a dance? Are you going to run from a fight?"

He snorted. "I think I'll let Colin and Fletcher handle the Casanova stuff."

Eden opened her mouth and forgot what she was going to say when headlights flashed through the trees lining the drive. Engines rumbled, and she was out of her chair and down the steps by the time Jay's truck pulled into sight, followed by Fletcher's car and a mid-sized U-Haul.

She ran across the yard and was waiting when Jay stopped the truck. Anxiety and relief bubbled up along with her power, and she hauled open the driver's side door and dragged Jay's head down for a blistering kiss.

He tumbled out and caught her around the waist, tugging her up off her feet. He met her kiss with more kissing, met her power with that wave of sweet, soothing magic she'd needed from the moment Kaley had fallen apart in her arms. The steadily building pressure vanished so fast her ears should have popped, and for a beautiful moment she floated on the release.

Then she just floated, her toes dangling inches above the ground as Jay turned his mouth to her ear. "Missed me, huh?"

"Just a little." She closed her eyes and rested her cheek against his. "Is everyone all right?"

He tensed in her arms. "Yeah. We'll talk about it later."

The screen door slammed, and Kaley walked out on the porch, her arms crossed over her chest. It was Eden's turn to tense as Zack took a few steps toward the house before shuddering to a halt.

Zack stared at Kaley. She stood, still as stone, expressionless. Jay lowered Eden to the ground as Mae eased toward Kaley, but no one spoke.

No one dared.

Finally Zack broke the silence by clearing his throat. "We brought the stuff you had in storage."

"Thank you," Kaley answered flatly.

Someone had to move before Kaley's control snapped. Eden eased out of Jay's arms and crossed the yard. "You boys leave the U-Haul for tomorrow and get cleaned up. We're sitting down to dinner together tonight." The steps creaked loudly in the silence as she climbed to stand next to Kaley. "Come on, honey. Will you help me set up the folding chairs?"

"I'll do it," the girl said, already turning toward the door. "You have other stuff going on."

An offer. A way out of having to choose between pack and family, between her cousin's sadness and a young woman's pain. The fact that it didn't feel like a choice at all might hurt later.

For now, it was painfully clear. Eden wrapped her arm around Kaley's shoulders and reached out to Mae. "The men can deal. I'm all yours."

Chapter Eight

Jay flipped the mattress into place and evened it on the box-spring platform with one leg. "There. How's it look?"

"Perfect." Eden tossed the fitted sheet onto the mattress and circled around to the opposite side. "Now I have beds in all the important places in town. My house, your house, above the diner and at the farm." She smiled up at him. "Or should I say *we* have beds."

As if there would be no question of them sharing said beds. Jay grinned. "Yes, we do."

"You like that, huh?" She tucked the sheet under the mattress and gave him an arch look. "You're the one with the no-sex rule. That witch better show up soon, that's all I'm saying."

"Didn't Shane tell you? They're due in today, the witch and her... Well, her bodyguard, for lack of a better word."

Eden froze with one hand tangled in the sheet. "Already? I thought it would take her some time to make arrangements."

Apparently, the alphas in Red Rock had felt there was no time to lose. "It's a good thing," he told her resolutely. She didn't need to hear that Stella's job would be to check them out as much as help.

"I know. I'm surprised, but mostly relieved." She straightened and rubbed her hands over her arms. "Maybe a little nervous. I've never met a witch."

"Not so different from anyone else until she starts breaking out the magic spells."

After she pulled the sheet smooth, Eden dropped to the bed and leaned back on her hands. "Lorelei mentioned something about spells for soundproofing. Is that something you're familiar with?"

With a house full of people with super senses, they'd soon have some pretty intimate privacy concerns. "I once knew a wizard who could make himself invisible when he was standing right in front of you. Couldn't smell him, either."

"I think everyone would appreciate a little protection from their super senses." She sank lower on the bed, bracing her weight on her elbows in a deceptively casual pose, an invitation that her eyes backed up. "I'm not making out with you in this bed if your friends are going to hear it."

"They're very, very good at ignoring things like that."

Her cheeks turned pink. "I may have a few kinks, but I'm pretty sure exhibitionism isn't one of them. I'm going to have a hard enough time with all the nakedness and shapeshifting when we get to the full moon."

Telling her that no one would pay any attention would do no good. He'd sure as hell be looking, and he didn't bother to hide his grin. "I bet you look damn good naked in the moonlight."

"You've already seen me naked," she reminded him, nudging his foot with hers. "Very unfair, since I can't say the same."

"If you're angling for me to drop trou, things aren't going to be very quiet in here."

She huffed and flopped back on the bed with a groan. "I know. I don't think I can spend too many more nights squirming in your lap without imploding. Does this Guide-bond thing take a long time?"

He'd only gone through the ceremony a few times. "Depends on your definition. Twenty minutes, maybe, once it's all set up?"

"Thank God. We're almost through this, right? Soon we might be able to stop for a little while and breathe?"

The words brought the fiasco in Memphis rushing back. "Shit, with those bastards in the city...who even knows?"

An engine rumbled in the distance, and Eden popped up and tilted her head. "That doesn't sound like my dad's truck," she said after a second of intent listening.

"No." Jay held out his hand for hers and walked out of the room, all the way out of the small house.

The dark truck that pulled down the driveway wasn't the same one from Memphis. For one, it had a bouncy woman with tawny blonde hair hanging out of the passenger window. "Hey there," she called out as the truck pulled to a stop.

Eden raised a hand. "Stella, I presume?"

She didn't even wait for the stern-faced man behind the wheel to shift into park before bounding out of the door. "Shane said this place was rustic, but I think it looks like a movie. Hi, yeah. I'm Stella."

"I'm Eden Green." She nudged Jay with her hip. "This is Jay."

"Ancheta," he supplied, holding out his hand.

The girl grabbed it. "Right on. Shane's friend."

The driver slammed his door and circled the vehicle, his movements slow and easy as his gaze flicked over each of them before continuing to take in both houses. Power flowed from him as he drew even with Stella. "I'm Keith Winston."

Jay took his hand. "Welcome to Clover."

Keith's grip was strong, but not so firm as to be challenging. He smiled as he released Jay's hand to clasp Eden's. "You must be the new wolf."

"Is it that obvious?" Eden asked, faking overdone dismay. "I haven't tried to sniff anyone in days."

"Well, that's no fun." He winked at her. "Jay, Eden, I'd like to thank you both a great deal for getting this troublemaker out of my hair."

"Don't mention it." Red Rock had its own witch, and could well afford to spare her apprentice. "How are Gavin and Sam?"

"Buried in honorary grandchildren and loving every minute of it." Keith rested a hand on Stella's shoulder. "I can only stay long enough to make sure Stella's settled, as a matter of fact. I've got a pair of twins celebrating their second birthday."

The blonde snorted. "If Daddy isn't there, Aunt Stella's the one who'll catch hell for it."

Eden laughed. "You've had a long trip from Montana. Come inside and I'll show you around. Anything to keep you out of trouble."

Two pots of coffee later, Jay had explained the situation to an increasingly somber Keith. Stella sat beside him, cursing and shaking her head until the dreadlocks framing her face swung into her eyes.

"It's ridiculous," she proclaimed. "Keith, come *on.*"

He clenched his jaw. "Jay's right. Most of the mess that went down in Helena happened because Joe and I took out the leaders of a corrupt pack and didn't think about what would rise in their place. They can't kill their way through the Memphis pack."

"And we don't want to," Jay added. "It's too much blood to be on anyone's hands, much less the people who came here. We just want peace."

Eden covered Jay's hand with her own. "Not just want it. They need it. They've been through too much."

Stella rose with another mutter. "I'm going to find Shane. I need a beer."

Jay stopped her. "Wait. Eden's a new wolf. I need some help setting up a Guide ceremony. As soon as possible, but definitely before the full moon."

"Yeah?" Stella propped a hand on her hip. "You two look pretty cozy. You gonna be her Guide?"

"Yes," Eden answered for both of them, her tone a little tart. "That's what I want."

"And that's what matters," Keith said firmly. "Stella, use the spell Sasha taught you. This isn't the time for fancy rituals."

"We could have a *little* decorum, couldn't we?" But she sighed and grabbed Jay's hand, then Eden's. Her eyes fluttered shut, and the air around them began to throb with power.

It didn't feel like a wolf. It didn't feel like anything Jay had experienced, not until the witch whispered a quiet incantation and the magic snapped like a string drawn too tight, lashing through the room.

When it settled, all Jay could feel was *Eden*. "That's it?"

Stella opened her eyes. "Standard three months. If it looks like I'm not going to be here at the end of it, I'll prepare a talisman that you can destroy to break the bond."

Eden stared blankly, her eyes wide and dazed. Through the bond, Jay could feel her wolf, stunned but rallying. Magic rose inside her, a wave that rushed down the newly opened connection before it could crest.

Exhaling in relief, she swayed.

"Oh, hell." Keith groaned and reached out a hand to catch Eden's shoulder. "First lesson—don't say fast if you don't mean *fast*. I should know better by now."

The witch blinked. "What'd I do?"

"My fault, Stella. I should have warned them." Keith patted Eden's shoulder as she steadied. "You're stronger than most, sweetheart. It'll take some time to grow into that power, but you will. If you ever need someone to talk to about it, Stella can tell you how to get in contact with my wife. She went through the same thing a few years ago."

Still looking a little dazed, Eden murmured her thanks. But under the table, her hand found Jay's and squeezed tight.

Stella saluted them with two fingers at her temple. "My pleasure. Now, if you don't mind..." She snatched up her bag. "I'm getting out of here. Little house, right?"

"That's where Shane is," Jay confirmed, three-quarters of his attention still fixed on Eden. Her fingertips traced teasing patterns over the back of his wrist, her skin warm.

She jumped when the door swung shut behind Stella and blinked at the witch's empty chair. Color flooded her cheeks. "I'm being a terrible host."

"She's used to wolves, honey. Right, Keith?"

Keith smiled and leaned back in his chair. "Stella will do just fine. She's used to living with wolves, and she's seen her share of trouble. She's been itching to get out on her own and flex her spellcasting muscles without her mentor staring over her shoulder, but Sasha wouldn't have sent her if she wasn't ready."

Jay dragged his focus back to the wolf sitting across from them. "Long term, what do we do about Memphis?"

"My advice?" Keith tapped his fingers on the table. "Try to find a spy, someone who can warn you if they're going to come. But either way...be ready for war. Have wards to protect those who can't fight, and train those who can. Have a plan in place so everyone knows which is which."

Zack might know someone left in Memphis who'd be willing to pass on information about the pack's movements, but even asking could put the would-be spy in mortal danger. "We have to expect them at any time. I've got some contacts through my job, but using them is a tricky, messy business."

"You're local law, aren't you?"

"I am."

"That'll help with the other problem, hopefully." Keith shook his head. "You're not as remote as I'd like, certainly not remote enough to be hidden away from humans like Red Rock. That'll be trouble if more refugees keep showing up."

It was a small town, and people had already been talking. "This place is a farm. Farms need labor, and little boutique organic outfits have been popping up all across the South over the last decade. As long as we keep our noses clean, we can make it work."

Keith smiled slowly. "Yeah, Stella told me about the alpaca business plan. She's a city girl with wide-eyed dreams about life on a farm. Don't shatter all her illusions on the first day."

"She's not our only former city dweller," Eden told him with an answering smile. She nudged Jay's foot with her own, rubbing their calves together under the table as her bright, innocent gaze stayed fixed on Keith. "I'll turn them all into country girls in no time."

Minx. "And if that fails, we'll keep them away from the creatures," Jay promised.

"At least the ones that might bite them," Eden said cheerfully.

Keith eyed her for a moment, then snorted. "Yeah, I forgot this part of the bonding too. I suppose it's inevitable."

"Lunch." Jay stood, keeping Eden's hand in his. "Can you at least stay for that before you have to head back?"

"Sure." Keith rose as well. "Where's Fletcher hiding himself? I haven't seen him in a year or more. Wanted to catch up before I roll out."

"He was out there with Shane earlier. Should still be."

"Good. You two get used to that bond now, while you have a chance."

Keith started for the door, and Eden must have had a moment of guilt. "We can walk you," she blurted out, giving Jay a helpless look. "It's only polite."

Keith snorted again. "Ancheta, time to teach your Initiate about priorities and pack...and how little use werewolves have for polite manners."

The door slammed behind their guest, and Jay picked Eden up and deposited her on the table. "What he means," he said slowly, "is that there's a time and place for everything...except when you're newly bonded."

She heaved out an unsteady breath and tangled her fingers in his shirt. "So the fact that I'm all tingly isn't just my own sexual frustration?"

"Common side effect." His voice came out too thick, almost hoarse.

One of Eden's hands squirmed under his shirt to brush his abdomen. "Are you tingly too?"

He'd been tingly for *days*, and he didn't bother to shield the edge of his lust from her. Instead, he slipped his hands into her hair, held her still—his gaze fixed on hers—and let her feel every pulse. Every heartbeat.

Her eyes flared gold. "You're under my skin," she whispered. Her fingers slid up his chest and brushed one nipple, and she sucked in a sharp breath when he let her feel his pleasure along with his lust. "Oh, this is *dirty*."

"Fringe benefit." He tipped her head back and scraped his teeth over her jaw. She shuddered and scratched his chest, her moan filling the kitchen.

He bit off a groan. The kitchen table was no place to seduce a woman—especially not for the first time—but it didn't matter. Not enough to make him stop.

Jay dragged her to the edge of the table, sliding her halfway astride his thigh. "Nothing dangerous about this now. Kiss me, and show me how you let go—"

Eden's mouth crashed into his, swallowing the last word. She rocked forward, riding his leg as her tongue drove in search of his.

He steadied her hips with one hand and slid the other up over her breast. Her top was made of some kind of thick chambray, but her nipple tightened in a heartbeat. She moaned again, a soft, hot sound that Jay coaxed into a lower, deeper noise by slipping free the first button on her shirt.

Two buttons later she tore her mouth from his, throwing her head back as she squirmed against his leg. "Oh God, oh *God.* This is insane. Why are you not as crazed as I am?"

He was burning, and the fact that she thought he might not be drew a ragged chuckle from this throat. "Control. Don't think about what I'm doing, Eden. Feel what I feel."

A heartbeat. Two. She exhaled on a shaky sigh as her fingers tangled in his hair. "You want to—to take me."

"Until there's no part of you that doesn't belong to me." Her shirt yielded under his hand, baring a white bra so sheer he could see her nipples, dusky against her pale skin. He bent his head and rocked her hips harder against his leg as he sucked one peak into his mouth.

Pleasure spiked. Tension spilled down their bond, and she slammed her wrist to her mouth to muffle a cry. Paying attention to the jolts sparking between them made it laughably easy to find the perfect rhythm, the speed and pressure that had her clutching at the edge of the table with one hand as she bit her wrist hard enough for him to feel it.

The wet mesh fabric clung to her nipple, and Jay gave her the slightest edge of teeth before turning his mouth to the flushed center of her chest. "That's it, honey. You'll feel so good coming all over me."

As if the words had been a command, her hips jerked. Her back bowed, arching over his arm until her hair pooled on the table. She came in virtual silence, her face slack and her lips parted on a soundless moan, but the intensity of it slammed into him as her wolf surged.

"Kaley, were you thinking of—" Lorelei walked into the kitchen, her eyes fixed on the catalog in her hand. She looked up and clapped one hand over her eyes before spinning around. "Oh shit. *Shit,* I'm sorry."

Eden sat up so fast she crashed into Jay as a choked squeal of embarrassment escaped her lips. Her cheeks flamed and she shoved at Jay's chest with clumsy hands. "No, no it's okay, we weren't—we were just—" She clutched the open edges of her shirt together, but her fumbling fingers popped the button off when she tried to fasten it. "*Fuck.*"

A slightly hysterical laugh bubbled out of Lorelei. "Yeah, I can tell."

Jay cleared his throat as he took over buttoning Eden's shirt. "The witch is here."

"She is?" Lorelei half-turned before snapping her head forward again. "Already?"

"Yeah." Eden finally met Jay's eyes, and embarrassment faded as her lips curved into a wry smile. "She's over at the little house with Shane. Once she made Jay my Guide, everyone fled. And now I'm understanding why."

"Uh-huh. I think I'm going to follow suit."

"We'll be out in a little bit," Eden promised.

There was no mistaking her look, and even as Lorelei hurried away, Jay shook his head. "Later, Eden."

Her breath hissed out. "I know. I *know*. But this is uncomfortably like being a teenager again. I just want enough privacy to get my damn hands on you."

"Tonight," he promised. The guys could take a hike for a few hours, maybe even until morning. He and Eden could be alone.

She shivered as he fastened the button over her breasts, and her eyelids drooped. "How do you do it?" she asked in a whisper. "If I couldn't feel you, I wouldn't think you were all that turned on. You're still giving me a complex."

The same way he did everything—because he had to. Because people were counting on him.

"Because it'll be worth it." He brushed her disheveled hair back from her face. In return, she turned her head to nuzzle his palm, her lips soft as they ran along his skin. A whisper, a quiet acceptance of his promise and an intimacy that went beyond sex.

Stopping was hell, but the tender way Eden touched him eclipsed all the discomfort. Knowing she wanted him just as much as he wanted her was soothing in its own way, turned a frantic rush toward pleasure into something more complex and rewarding. A chase in every sense of the word—stop and go, back and forth, but when they finally managed to catch one another...

The chase would end, and hell would turn to heaven in a heartbeat.

Chapter Nine

Eden had assumed the warmth and arousal of her new bond with Jay would fade eventually.

She'd been half-right.

Lunch was long behind them, and the men and women had parted ways for the afternoon's work. Only practical when Mae still froze up when confronted with Jay or Shane and outright avoided Colin and Fletcher, but the division of the genders made the farm feel a little stuck in time. Eden could hear the men in the distance through the open back door, the pounding of hammers and occasional buzz of a saw interspersed with thuds and grunts. Masculine sounds, sharply contrasting with the bright chaos of yarn and crafting materials littering every surface of the kitchen.

It might have perturbed her more if Shane and Fletcher hadn't seemed perfectly willing to sort yarn and package decorative soaps alongside the women. Respect had the males keeping their distance, not disdain or antiquated notions of gender roles. And no matter how far they strayed from the house, Eden could track Jay's presence, a warm awareness that brought whispers of emotion along with a steady embrace of soothing power.

She wasn't alone anymore. The knowledge made the ground solid under her feet again, and the shards of glass tearing up her throat had vanished. With a little time and luck, maybe they could make that true for all of Zack's pack.

Eden opened the next box in her stack and inhaled the scent of lemon and lavender. "Is this lotion?"

"Body cream," Kaley offered with a grin. "Mae's skin-care specialty."

"*Our* specialty," Mae corrected, tucking a strand of pink hair behind her ear. "Kaley's pretty much responsible for all the most popular scents. She has good instincts."

Eden lifted one professionally labeled jar declaring *all natural ingredients* in a clean, elegant font. "How much profit do you make per jar?"

"With that? A few dollars wholesale, a little more retail. I was working on an online storefront when..." Mae trailed off and shoved her hands into the pockets of Shane's hoodie. She'd taken to wearing it instead of a jacket, and no one had commented on it, not even to tease.

Undoubtedly no one wanted to risk taking away the small comfort Mae had found. Eden filled the awkward silence by lifting the box. "So which scent is your favorite, Kaley?"

"Sultry Southern Nights." She reached over and dug through a box until she came up with a bottle, which she handed to Eden. "It has jasmine and vanilla, with a little bit of amber and musk."

The scent matched the name, heavy and sensual. Eden could imagine the jars lining shelves at a boutique in Memphis and selling in bulk to tourists who wanted to take a little bit of the South home with them. "This is amazing, y'all. I thought you had more of an idea than an honest-to-God business already underway."

Her approval brought a hint of color to Mae's cheeks. "It's really thanks to Kaley and Lorelei. They encouraged me to make it more than a hobby. I started off only selling the yarn, but the bath and body products are really popular." She shifted awkwardly and offered Eden a shy whisper of a smile as Stella walked into the kitchen and eyed the products scattered across the table.

"Organic plays big with the hipster demographic." Stella sniffed at an open jar and hummed. "So what's the deal with your cousin, Eden? He's cute, got that whole motorcycle-gang thing happening. Taken?"

Tension snapped through the kitchen. The friendly light in Mae's eyes vanished, replaced by something cold and protective. Kaley was sorting bottles as if her life depended on it, all her attention focused on placing lotions and face creams into battered woven baskets.

"It's complicated," Eden told the witch carefully. "He's been through a lot and could use some space." The pounding of the hammers from outside had fallen silent, and Eden winced. "Plus, he's probably listening to this conversation."

Stella shrugged, clearly unembarrassed by the possibility. "You never know if you don't ask, right?"

The hammering started again with renewed enthusiasm, and Eden bit her lip against a smile. "I'm still hung up on the human idea of privacy being possible. Doesn't work so well among werewolves, I guess."

"Jay mentioned privacy wards. I can do that, you know. Magical soundproofing." She shrugged again. "No one in Red Rock would dare live without it."

Eden carried the box of body cream over to the table where Kaley had started sorting bars of soap. "What about in Memphis? Did y'all have anything like that?"

It took Kaley a moment to answer. "Aside from a few people who roomed together, we lived apart. We only—"

A scream of sheer animal panic tore through the house. Eden acted on instinct, lunging from the table with a burst of inhuman speed. Her chair toppled over in slow motion, clattering to the kitchen floor as she reached the bottom of the stairs.

So fast, and not fast enough. There had been so much terror in that scream, so much *pain*. She stumbled on the steps, awkward as werewolf agility and human muscle memory did uncomfortable battle.

She clawed her way up the final two stairs and burst into the upstairs sitting room. Lorelei stood in front of Quinn's open bedroom door, her hand clapped to her mouth, her shoulders shaking.

Dread overtook any other emotion. Eden froze, knowing both that she had to face that open door and that she wasn't prepared for what she'd find on the other side. Behind her, the stairs shook under a stampede of footsteps, a wave of concern that washed her forward, ready or not.

She wasn't. She couldn't be. But the others had followed, were already at her back, a flood of agitated power converging on her from all directions. Steeling her spine, she crossed to Lorelei's side.

Quinn swung from an exposed rafter in the ceiling, the rope he'd looped around his neck digging into his skin. His face was swollen, purple, his tongue protruding slightly from his mouth. Eden looked away. She had no idea how long he'd been there, but one thing was clear.

He was dead.

Lorelei gasped in a breath as Kaley, Mae and Stella stumbled into the room behind them. "No, get out of here. Don't look."

Eden grabbed for the door and hauled it shut as her stomach threatened to revolt. "Jay," she choked out. "We need to get everyone back downstairs and find Jay."

"Where's Quinn?" Kaley demanded. "Eden, what's going on?"

She parked herself in front of the door like a sentinel and raised her voice. "Quinn's—" What could she say? There was no way to soften this blow and no reason to wait. She didn't need Jay to confirm what she'd seen. But she couldn't get the words out, couldn't make her lips form them.

She couldn't even say them in the silent darkness of her own mind.

Jay appeared at the top of the stairs. "We heard a scream."

Lorelei herded Mae and Kaley past him, her face pale and her hands shaking. "You heard Eden. Downstairs, now. Let them—let them do what they have to do."

Mutters. Protests. But they obeyed, slipping down the steps, and then there was only Jay. Strong, steady Jay, but not even he could make this all right. Eden wet her lips, tasted salt, and realized she'd started crying. "It's Quinn," she whispered. "I think he killed himself."

"*What?*" He laid his hand on her shoulder as he walked past, but turned her away before opening Quinn's door. "Fuck," he muttered. "Oh, Jesus."

Looking away didn't help. The image of Quinn's still body had painted itself on the backs of her eyelids in a thousand vivid colors. "We should have heard something. We should have checked on him when we *didn't.*"

"You can't watch everyone all the time." The door closed, and Jay wrapped his arms around her. "Shit, what do we do?"

"I don't know." Numbness was settling over her, the kind she'd always told herself was practical. In a crisis, things needed to be done, and it was easier to deal with the practicalities if you couldn't feel. But what practicalities were there when a werewolf took his own life?

She clutched at Jay's arm and tried to walk through the possibilities. "If this had happened somewhere else, I'd be calling 911. Can werewolves even do that?"

"He's dead," Jay whispered. "No one who looks at him now will ever know he wasn't human. With something like this, the

Medical Examiner is supposed to do an autopsy, make sure it really *was* a..." He trailed off. "It'll mean more gossip."

Eden stiffened as she imagined nosy neighbors sneaking onto the farm to uncover illicit activity—and discovering something far more damning. "We can't afford much more, can we?"

"No," he admitted. "But burying him out back like a fucking dog might be even worse for the rest of them. We need to talk to Zack, see what he thinks."

Ice crept through her veins, helping with the numbness. "No one's burying anyone like a dog. Even if Zack wants to keep it quiet, we can do it with compassion. We can do it properly."

"You're right. I didn't mean—"

Footsteps thumped up the stairs, and Colin walked in. His gaze raked over Eden before jumping past her to land on Jay. "Which do you want me to manage, the dead or the living?"

Jay shuddered. "Get in there and get him down."

"I'll help," Stella offered hurriedly.

Colin's expression looked as flat as Eden felt. "Zack's at the foot of the stairs," he said as he circled them. "I'm not sure if he's waiting for you or guarding the way up."

"I'm on it." Jay pulled Eden away from Quinn's door. "Come on. I need you to help me with him."

It didn't seem like a monumental request, not until she reached the bottom step and Zack turned to face her. If she was numb, he was...empty. No, worse. Empty implied a passive, neutral state. Zack was folding in on himself, forming a black hole that swallowed emotion before it could form. Empty could be filled, fixed, but the darkness inside Zack might hollow out anyone who tried.

He looked over her shoulder, at Jay. "How'd he do it?"

"It doesn't matter," Jay said quietly. "Did he have family?"

Zack shook his head. "None that knew he was still alive. He broke ties when he was turned, more than ten years ago."

"Then we need to think about whether to get the authorities involved, or just have a quiet burial and take care of him as best we can."

Zack stared in silence for so long that Eden reached out to him. He flinched back and refocused on Jay. "If there's any chance the authorities might end up looking into the rest of us, it's not worth it. We've all got too much weird shit to explain."

Jay nodded. "Then it needs to be tonight. I'll take care of the practicalities."

Zack closed his eyes. "So now there are four of us. Not much of a pack."

"Six," Jay corrected firmly. "Eden and I are right here."

"And none of us are going anywhere," Eden promised. As soon as the words escaped her lips she regretted them. With her body as numb as her heart, the words rang hollow.

She didn't believe them. No one was going anywhere, but Zack was still slipping away. He didn't have to make Quinn's choice to leave. If something didn't change, that hungry emptiness inside her cousin would consume every trace of the man he'd become.

Something had to change. Soon.

They buried Quinn in a small clearing surrounded by trees near the center of the farm. Stella laid protective wards around its perimeter while Fletcher and Colin dug the grave deep into the loamy soil.

The magic tickled over Jay's senses as they crossed the barrier, raising the hairs on the back of his neck. It had been too long since he'd been involved in the harsh reality of being a wolf in human society, too long since he'd dealt with anything but his own practical matters. And, since reaching adulthood, those were few—he had good control, never had to worry about hurting anyone or blowing his cover.

Never had to worry about much of anything until now.

Horrible, to be burying someone in the middle of the night by the light of the moon. No preachers, no funeral service or sleek caskets, none of the sterile niceties that allowed you to remove yourself from the proceedings. With the mounds of dirt excavated from the grave covered by bright green plastic carpeting, it was easy to see only the steel box being lowered into the cold ground.

All they had was a body sewn into a sheet from the attic.

But as he looked at the somber, sometimes tear-streaked faces around him, the truth hit him. They didn't need tact. They needed the visceral candor of this moment—no music, no flowers, no sonorous prayer offered by a religious official.

Just them and their dead friend.

Someone had to say something, but a wind warmer than the chilly night breeze rushed past him, odd enough to draw his attention. It felt like *breath*, and Jay turned instinctively, looking for its source.

Nothing. No one behind him, just the quiet of the night.

The whole damn thing was making him paranoid.

The wolves gathered in a ragged circle around the grave. Mae, Kaley and Lorelei huddled together, a quiet knot of pain echoed in the tight set of Zack's shoulders as he stood stiffly beside them.

No one spoke. No one seemed able to.

Jay cleared his throat and squeezed Eden's hand. "I didn't know Quinn, but I wish... Well, I wish the things he'd been through hadn't seemed so insurmountable."

Mae sniffled and turned her face to Lorelei's shoulder. Fletcher looked away from the women, as if their obvious pain was too much—or too naked—to bear.

A hand brushed Jay's right shoulder. He glanced back again. There was no one behind him, and Eden stood close to his left side, her right hand tucked into both of his.

Paranoid.

Kaley wiped her red eyes and stepped forward. Shane tried to stop her, but Zack growled a low warning. She shook her head and wrapped her hands around the pitted wooden handle of a shovel. "I need to do this."

Fletcher retrieved a second shovel. "We can do it together. Anyone who wants to."

Mae looked like she wanted to be doing *anything* else. Eden and Lorelei led her away from the open grave as Jay picked up a shovel.

When the first clump of dirt hit the wrapped bundle at the bottom of the grave, a sob tore through the night. At first, Jay thought it was Kaley, but her features were set in a grim, determined mask as she worked. It echoed again, decidedly feminine—and too close to be any of the other women. Jay froze, but no one else seemed to have heard it.

He was losing his fucking mind.

Colin hesitated, his dirt-laden shovel hovering over the grave. "You okay, Ancheta?"

Stress, nothing more. "Yeah, I'm square."

Colin didn't seem to believe him, but he returned to shoveling. With five werewolves working in focused silence, the grave filled quickly. Eden reappeared when they were half-done, her bare arms pale under the nearly full moon. She'd stripped off her jacket and filled it with dozens of moss-covered rocks of various sizes. "Mae wants to build something to mark the grave."

Jay's protest caught in his throat. Marking the grave made it recognizable, suspicious.

Shane leaned on the handle of his shovel. "I bet Stella can add redirection to the wards. Make it so people who don't know this place is here just won't notice."

"If it could be safe..." Eden's eyes held a quiet plea. "She can say goodbye in her own way."

Jay relented. "It's fine. Does she need help?"

Eden glanced at the grave and shook her head. "It'll take a few more trips this way...but that's all right. You'll be done before she gets back."

And they were. As Fletcher and Shane rounded off the mound of dirt, Kaley rubbed a grimy hand across her forehead and knelt to help Mae sort through the rocks she'd gathered. Jay collected the shovels and headed back toward the barn.

They didn't need him to construct a cairn for their friend. It wasn't his place.

"What's this?" Shane asked, blocking out the moonlight as he loomed over the fire pit.

Jay placed one last log. "Didn't want to be in the house just now. Thought I'd build a fire instead."

Colin appeared at Shane's side. "Mind some company?"

"Depends," Shane said as he settled next to Jay. "Did you bring beer?"

"Better." He pulled a flask out of his jacket. "Moonshine. Seems fitting."

Jay snorted. "If you want to go blind, maybe."

"Only temporarily." Colin took a sip before offering the flask to Shane. "Can't get a buzz off beer, and tonight I could use one."

"That's what this is for." A crate of bottles rattled in Stella's arms as she rounded the growing fire. "I heard there were dry counties in this godforsaken state, so I brought my own. Tonight's as good a night as any to drain it all."

Colin choked on his moonshine and coughed. "Damn. Gotta love a woman who brings her own liquor cabinet wherever she goes. How'd you become friends with a stick-in-the-mud like Shane?"

"He saved my life, that's how." She retrieved a sleeve of red plastic cups from the crate and waved them. "Who wants one?"

Jay held out a hand. "Got any bourbon?"

"Does the Pope shit in the woods?"

"I should think not," Eden murmured from behind Jay. She slid to the ground next to him and snuggled into his side. "How undignified for the Pope."

"Maybe if he's camping." He wrapped an arm around her. "Everything okay inside?"

"I think so. I made sure all three of them got something to eat." She turned her face to his shoulder and closed her eyes. "That's all I can do, isn't it? Give them time."

Impossible to know for sure. They'd only just met—even Eden and her cousin, in a way—and their only option was to rely on instinct. "We can be here if they need us. That's it."

Eden ignored the whispers from the other side of the fire and slipped her hand into Jay's. "It doesn't feel like enough." Unspoken was her obvious grief—for Quinn, it *hadn't* been enough.

"It isn't, but our only other choice is to force them. They've had enough of that."

"I know, you're right. They need—" She cut off as the back door swung shut with a soft *thud*. The porch stairs creaked under Mae's slow, wary steps. Eden shifted as if to stand, but after a moment settled back against Jay's side and clutched his hand as they waited for Mae to come to them—on her own terms.

Stella turned, following their gazes, and held up a bottle. "Want some?"

Mae hesitated for an awkward moment, her gaze taking in the wolves around the fire. Jay couldn't tell if it was the woman or the wolf who took the first step, but it was a submissive in desperate need of pack who edged into the spot Stella made for her. She accepted the bottle with a shy smile. "Thanks. I could use a drink."

"You and me both, sister."

Mae took a swig from the bottle and stared into the fire. "I just wanted to say...I know you guys tried. Are trying. Thanks for helping us."

Shane stared down into his cup. "I want to know something about Quinn. Anything."

"Quinn was..." She picked at the edge of the label on the bottle. "He was funny. Witty. He had this dry, sarcastic sense of humor. Half the time, people weren't sure if he was serious or making a joke."

"He played guitar." Lorelei stepped out of the shadows near the corner of the house. "For a while, he wanted to go to Nashville. Be a star."

Instead, he'd wound up getting the shit kicked out of him in Memphis. Jay drained his drink and leaned over to pull a new bottle from the crate next to Stella's feet.

"He used to tease us by writing silly little songs." Mae shifted aside to make room for Lorelei. "I always loved everyone else's and groaned through mine."

Lorelei dropped beside her and sniffed through a laugh. "Remember when he was writing the one about Zack and spent a week trying to think of something clever that rhymed with *surly buttface*?"

Mae's lips twitched. "And Kaley and I kept trying to help him, but he didn't like *twirly mutt race* or *girly smut phase.*"

The back door slammed again. "That's because we're horrible lyricists." Kaley stepped off the porch, a cardboard six-pack of beer in one hand. "Then again, so was Quinn."

Eden nudged Jay to make room for Kaley, completing the ragged circle around the fire. "What did Quinn do when he wasn't singing?" she asked as she accepted a beer.

"Before everything went to hell?" Kaley asked. "He made everyone laugh. After? He kept his head down and tried not to make trouble, just like the rest of us."

Mae protested with a soft noise. "He didn't just keep his head down. He could have, and they might have left him alone, but he did what he could. Checked up on me. Made sure I was okay, even when it put him in danger."

Kaley didn't answer, and a closer look at the girl's slightly out-of-focus eyes told Jay plenty. The six-pack might've been her second of the night already, even the third.

He topped off his drink. "A toast?"

Lorelei lifted her cup with a smile. "For Quinn."

"Quinn," Mae whispered, her voice hoarse. The others followed suit, sipping from glass bottles and plastic cups and Colin's silver flask. The fire crackled, sending sparks up into the sky, and that warm air ghosted across the back of Jay's neck again.

At his side, Eden shivered, and he tightened his arm around her. "For Quinn," he said.

Zack was nowhere to be found, and a single light burned in the bedroom Fletcher had claimed in the little house. They both had their reasons for not joining the pack around the fire, reasons no one could argue with or counter.

All the rest of them could do was be there.

Chapter Ten

Eden woke to the sun slanting over her face at an odd angle and her pulse kicking viciously inside her skull. She was sprawled on top of the blankets but half under Jay, the illicitness of their tangled limbs undercut by the fact that they were both fully clothed.

Her mouth tasted like cotton. Her body tingled. Opening her eyes increased the throbbing in her head, so Eden clenched them shut and burrowed farther under Jay, all too ready to hide from the morning.

It was totally unfair that werewolves could get hangovers.

His arm tightened around her waist, steely and immovable. "Too early for squirming," he growled.

Eden stilled as her wolf rose, swift and hungry, as enraged by Jay's gruff command as she was seduced by his show of strength. This wasn't a spike of unbridled power that could spill down their bond and dissipate. The urge to challenge him lived in every atom of her being. It *was* her.

Snarling, she whipped her head around and bit his shoulder.

"Ow." He laughed and rolled to his back, rubbing his shoulder. "Feeling feisty, honey?"

Eden surged over him, straddling his hips before bracing her hands on either side of his head. Her disheveled hair fell around both of them, a blonde tangle that smelled of last night's bonfire. The fire was still burning inside her, smoke and flame and everything wild. "I feel—" What word encompassed this? What *could*?

His amusement faded as he stroked his hands up her thighs. "You're already feeling the moon."

"Am I?" She scraped her nails down the bronze skin of his arm, pressing harder until white lines rose in the wake of her fingers. Marks. Possession. "I don't know if I want to fight or—" At any other time she might have blunted the truth, but today only one word fit. "Fuck."

"Or both?" He flipped her suddenly, pinning her to the mattress with her hands above her head. "Can you even separate them right now, with the moon so close?"

No. It was too terrifying to admit, too alien. She bucked up with all her newly won strength, and it wasn't a game. She wanted to twist free, wanted to rake her nails over his skin and bite him again, wanted him to tear open her clothes and shove her against the bed—

She whimpered and tried to force the lurid fantasy from her mind. "This is kind of perverse."

He didn't argue. Instead, he bent his head to hers, nuzzling her cheek and the spot just below her ear.

Gentle and soft. A trap, and she tumbled into it, craning her neck back in silent encouragement. "My skin is too tight. My clothes are too."

His soothing hum vibrated against the sensitive skin at the base of her throat. "We have a bond now. Give a little of it to me."

"I don't think she wants me to." She tugged at his grip, wriggling her wrists as irritation and arousal rose in equal measure. "Can you take it?"

"It doesn't work that way." He gripped both of her wrists with one hand and lowered the other to her cheek, brushing her tangled hair back from her face.

His eyes glowed. Gold, beautiful, flaring with the same fire that licked inside her skin. Power curled around her, pressing in as her wolf struggled out. As fierce as she felt, the unshakable strength inside him burned brighter. Hotter.

She couldn't meet his eyes, so she squeezed hers shut as Jay stroked over her, around her, inside her. A touch beyond that of flesh, and her wolf yielded with an irritated murmur, leaching the tension from Eden's body. "Oh..."

"See?" Just a whisper, softer than the power that encircled them both. "We don't take. We give."

Yesterday, she'd sprawled on this bed and worried about the supernatural senses of the men sleeping upstairs. Now, with her wolf so close to the surface, modesty seemed a foreign concept. "But I want you to take me."

A tiny shudder ran through him, and he captured her mouth with a low groan. Thrilled by the fracture in his self-control, Eden licked his lips and tangled her legs around his, using the only leverage she had with her hands still pinned.

His tongue rubbed over hers, a gentle tease, and his groan was more growl when she opened wider to let him in. He rocked his hips against hers, reached down to grip her leg and pull it higher on his body.

The wolf struck without warning, taking advantage of Jay's moment off balance. Eden slammed her heel into the bed and rolled them both as hard as she could, fighting for the top, for dominance, for that thrilling moment of hovering over him—

Only a moment. Momentum propelled them in a tangle of limbs, and Eden choked on a startled shriek as they tumbled to the floor.

Jay gasped and shook, his eyes squeezed shut. After a heartbeat, his suppressed laughter bubbled out in a breathless chuckle. "Well. That didn't exactly go as planned."

Eden rolled off him and scrubbed a hand over her face. Her body still throbbed, but she couldn't tell if the need riding her would be satisfied by sex—at least, not by the sort of sex she was used to having. "I want to..." His chuckle dwindled, and she missed it. Craved it. "I want to play."

He propped his elbow on the floor and rested his head on his hand. "That's what the full moon is for. We'll run, play. It's about the wolf, the *pack*."

"The needs are getting all mixed up." Facing him, she traced a finger down the row of buttons on his plaid shirt. "That's just because it's you, right? I like everyone else, but I don't want to play the same kinds of games with them."

"I hope not." He caught her hand and held it, even as he slipped free the button under their fingers with his thumb.

Eden pushed herself to her knees with a grace she was starting to enjoy possessing. It made her feel more seductive as she inched down his body until her head was even with his hips. "Are you going to let me play games with you?"

Someone pounded on the door, followed quickly by Colin's voice. "Everything okay? I heard a crash."

Groaning, Eden dropped her head to Jay's stomach. "I hate life."

Jay drove his hands into her hair with a sigh. "First full moon with new alphas? It's a big day. They're going to need us."

Colin obviously agreed. He cleared his throat loudly on the other side of the door. "Okay, I take it you're both fine. There's coffee in the kitchen and I'll get out of here, but people are already up and moving at the big house. Fair warning."

"We're on our way," Jay called. He climbed to his feet and helped Eden up. "Breakfast, or Advil and water?"

Her stomach rumbled, and her head still hurt. "All three, I think."

He grinned. "Something tells me there's going to be a lot of that this morning."

She scrunched up her nose and tried for an expression of annoyance, but God knew he was right. Colin had started sharing his teeth-fuzzying moonshine between the stories about Quinn and the tears, and everyone had had enough of it to blunt the edges of pain.

Everyone except Zack.

Willfully pushing aside her worry for her cousin, Eden straightened her clothes and ran her fingers through her tousled hair, trying to comb it into something respectable enough for breakfast. "My hangover's fading pretty fast. It's the rest of it I'm worried about. Sniffing people is bad enough. I don't want to start pouncing on people just because my wolf's feeling...frolicsome."

"You'll get straight soon enough." Jay buttoned his shirt and grabbed his boots from the foot of the bed. "Come on. I think I smell pancakes and sausage."

She could, too, but faint enough that it had to be coming from the big house. She found her sneakers where Jay had dumped them the night before and followed him out of the bedroom, then through the French doors in the kitchen.

The main farmhouse rose up against the bright morning sky, less ominous in the daylight than it had been last night, when liquor and darkness had combined to bring ghosts to life. She'd gotten more than one chill when ghostly fingers shivered up her spine or she caught movement out of the corner of her eye. Easily blamed on the moonshine...

And yet.

Eden's foot came down on a twig with a *crack* that startled her back to the present. Shivering, she wrapped an arm through Jay's and pressed closer to his side. "I guess I proved one thing last night."

"What's that?"

"That you were right," she said softly. "I'm strong enough to do this. If I made it through yesterday...I think I can do this."

"Good." He kissed the top of her head. "Because I wasn't kidding. They're going to need you."

The words felt right. They resonated with a part of her that was already too comfortable back on the farm. "You'll have to help me figure out the day. What do the alphas do for the pack during the full moon?"

"Keep everyone safe while they let loose for a little while. Show them that they *can* let loose."

"So we run and we play?"

"The flip side of banding together for protection and survival. Another benefit of social structure."

It sounded better than she'd expected, like coming home to a place where she belonged, with people who understood her. After a lifetime of judiciously editing the truth about her family and her childhood, it sounded like freedom.

"You haven't had any of that." Eden stopped short of the steps leading up to the wrap-around porch and peered at Jay. "Was it hard, living without it?"

He looked away for a moment before finally meeting her eyes. "It's harder *and* it's easier. Hard to have to keep to yourself all the time, hide the reality of who and what you are. But being with other wolves—unless they're absolutely, without a doubt, the *right* ones... It's impossible to make it work without everyone understanding what's right, what their place is and accepting that."

Zack hadn't been the only one to avoid the gathering at the fire last night. "Fletcher can't stay, can he? He won't fit."

A flash of pain clouded Jay's eyes. "No, we've been through it before. Eventually, he'll have to go."

Eden smoothed her hand over his cheek, protectiveness blooming inside her until it overtook the itch of the moon. "I'm sorry."

"Nothing to be sorry about. It just is."

It felt a little bit like a warning, but she wasn't sure she wanted to ask. She was too afraid the conversation would lead to Zack. Broken Zack, who couldn't survive the way he was, but might not fit if he became whole again. "It doesn't matter today," she said, half-begging him to agree.

He shook his head as he pulled her up the steps. "No, not today."

Breakfast turned into brunch, which gave way to lunch without much pause. Everyone seemed as energized as Eden felt, and barely restrained energy apparently translated to boundless hunger in werewolves.

Someone had thrown the kitchen doors open to the autumn sun. Eden poured sweet tea into an ice-filled mason jar and watched through the window as Kaley tackled Colin, rolled, and came up with the football clutched triumphantly in one hand.

"How long has he known Colin?" Lorelei asked. "Jay, obviously."

"Over a decade." Eden bit back a smile as Colin grumbled, his dangerous edge muted by the good-natured humor in his eyes. Mae might still be wary, but Colin's grumpy-older-brother routine had worked its magic on Kaley.

"They've all been friends a long time," Eden continued, turning to face Lorelei. "Colin travels a lot, from what I've gathered. This is the first time he's stayed still in a while."

"I've heard of him. What he does, I mean." Lorelei finished slicing a lemon and dropped the whole thing in the tea pitcher.

"Then you may know more than me. Jay only told me that Colin used to deal with corrupt alphas." *Deal with* was such a sterile way of putting it, but it was hard to reconcile the man playing football in the back yard with a trail of vigilante killings that had started before Eden had graduated from college.

"They call them enforcers. They can work for alphas as part of a pack, or they can strike out on their own." Lorelei flashed her an apologetic look. "I've been picking Shane's brain—and borrowing his laptop. There's too much I don't know, and that's unacceptable."

An idea Eden needed to steal. "We should start a study group. I've asked Jay most of my questions, but I'm still struggling to understand the basic stuff. What everything I'm feeling means, when it's going to get better..."

"It couldn't hurt for everyone to learn. Our experiences—" She broke off and looked away. "Zack tried, but it was obvious he hadn't had the easiest or best time of it, either."

No, he couldn't have, even being born to the life. "I don't know how much his mother taught him before she disappeared. It must have been hard for him, though. There was no one here who understood."

Lorelei laid a hand on Eden's shoulder. "He's going to be okay. Once he gets used to not being scared."

"I know." Eden reached for Lorelei's hand, and hope surged when the other woman didn't pull away. "How are you doing? You're the one holding everyone else together."

"It seems worse than it is. There have been a lot of good times, and we all lean on each other."

It was beyond stupid to feel a stab of longing, but everyone at Green Pines had history. Stories. Jay and his friends, Zack and his pack. Eden squeezed Lorelei's hand lightly before turning to retrieve her tea. "Tell me a story about a good time. About Zack."

"Zack?" She leaned against the counter and crossed her arms over her chest. "He lets Kaley and Mae get away with anything. One time, we were hanging out in this bar in

Riverside, and the girls were at the pool table. These guys came up, thinking they'd be easy marks, so Kaley and Mae started hustling them. Pretty soon, the guys were five hundred bucks in the hole and mad as hell."

Eden could picture it all too easily—Kaley's farm-girl cheerfulness, and Mae with her dreamy artist demeanor. They'd be able to coast on cute smiles and "beginner's luck" long enough to get rich. "I can guess how Zack features into this."

"Mmm, growled until the guys paid up and made sure the situation didn't get ugly." Lorelei caught Eden's gaze. "But that's what he does—what he *did*. People look at Zack and think he gets off on violence, but I've only seen him try anything and everything to avoid it."

It was the way Eden had remembered him too. "You know him better than I do. I think he has trouble looking at me sometimes. He knew me as a scrawny, angry ten-year-old."

"Maybe. But you're not that anymore."

"Eventually he'll notice." Eden smiled and poked the generous curve of her hip. "Not scrawny, and not ten. I still have a temper, though, and I'm not sure becoming a werewolf has helped that."

"Yeah, well, what are you gonna do?" Lorelei shrugged and nodded toward the open back door. "When in doubt, play football."

Football wouldn't scratch the itch. Eden took a long sip of her tea before checking the clock above the sink. "Do we usually wait until sunset before we do the...wolf stuff?"

"Change? It's safer most places, I guess. The call doesn't get too overwhelming until later, when the moon is really high and bright..." Lorelei trailed off, an almost wistful expression overtaking her features.

"The call. Is that what this is? It's the oddest feeling." Her cheeks heated as she rubbed a hand over her arm. "And I get really confused when I'm around Jay. That's why I'm not playing football."

Lorelei wrinkled her nose with a soft chuckle. "Confused? Really?"

Eden groaned and covered her eyes. "Okay, how crazy I get is the confusing part. I'm not used to being so—so unrestrained."

"Uh-huh. I'm sure you'll make out okay."

"So there aren't any surprises I need to know about? Any weird werewolf sex stuff my new boyfriend forgot to tell me?"

Lorelei blinked at her. "I'm a werewolf and I have sex, but I'm not sure that makes me an expert on the subject."

Maybe her lack of friends had nothing to do with the dark secrets of her childhood. Maybe she was just socially hopeless. "I don't need a sex expert. I need—"

Colin cleared his throat loudly from the doorway, causing Eden to start. "I don't know where that sentence is going," he said, his lips twitching as if he was fighting a smile, "but I figured you'd want to know I was here before you finished it."

Lorelei tilted her head and regarded him thoughtfully. "Women have sex. Women *like* sex. That can't be a foreign concept for a man like you."

Both of Colin's eyebrows swept up as he crossed his arms over his solid chest, his gaze fixed on Lorelei with such intent focus that Eden felt like a piece of kitchen furniture. "And what sort of man is that?" he asked softly.

"You're the goddamn Batman." She smiled. "I thought you knew."

Colin stared at her like he couldn't quite believe—or understand—what she'd just said. No amount of self-control could save Eden. She slapped her hand over her mouth and tried—*tried* to hold back laughter.

It bubbled up even stronger when Colin shot her a disgruntled look. "Jay wanted me to tell you both that it's almost time to go running. We're going to clear out early so Stella can get to work on the soundproofing wards."

He looked so perplexed, like he wasn't used to being laughed at by women. With those dark, brooding eyes and his bad-boy vibe, he probably wasn't. Eden tried to have a care for his manly ego as she choked back her giggles and nodded solemnly. "Thank you, Colin."

Lorelei blinked innocently as he watched them both with an expression caught between grumpy and wary, but when he turned to go, her gaze swept over him, all traces of humor gone. "He needs someone to loosen him up."

Colin hesitated for a heartbeat before muttering something under his breath. He disappeared out the door, and Eden listened to his boots clomp across the porch. Irritation, but no real temper. The weaker wolves were safe with Colin, even if they did poke at his ego.

But Lorelei was watching him storm away like she couldn't tear her gaze from his ass, which reminded Eden of a different sort of safety the women were guaranteed. "Jay made it pretty clear to all of them that there was to be no...loosening up. At least not before y'all are settled and the bad stuff is long behind us."

"Did he? Interesting."

"None of them seem the type to chase a woman who doesn't want to be chased, but Jay's serious about making this a safe place." Eden returned the tea to the fridge before grinning at Lorelei. "That means all the chasing is up to you."

"I'm not chasing anyone." Lorelei tugged at the back door, holding it open for Eden. "It was just an observation."

"Mmm." Eden didn't push. She slipped through the door and almost bumped into Jay on the porch. His proximity roused the prickles under her skin as quickly as his touch soothed them, and she leaned against his chest for one indulgent moment. "Is it time?"

"Yeah." He stroked a hand over her hair, and she felt the gentle questing of magic. "You're ready."

She felt the words in her bones, bones that would snap soon enough. Twist, change... Pain was nearly the only thing she remembered from the first time. Pain, and Jay's warmth around her. "I'm a little scared."

"We'll go someplace alone, if you want. Just us." Beyond him, out at the edge of the blackened circle where they'd built the bonfire, Kaley tugged her shirt over her head and let it fall.

At some point, Eden would have to grow used to the casual nudity. Kaley wasn't the only one stripping off her clothes. Fletcher unbuttoned his shirt to reveal a tanned chest. Colin, already naked above the waist, tugged at his belt as he muttered something to Shane, and even Mae seemed unbothered. She stood next to Lorelei in jeans and a bra, showing off an intricate tattoo of flowers and vines encircling her waist.

Eden tucked her face against Jay's chest. "Maybe this first time. I don't know if I'm ready for an audience."

He grasped her hand and tugged her off the porch. "We'll be around shortly," he announced. "If there's trouble or you need us...just howl."

A couple of the wolves smiled. Someone murmured encouragement—Mae, or maybe Kaley. Eden barely heard it.

Her wolf knew it was time.

Every step away from the farm pushed anticipation higher and wrapped nerves tighter until she couldn't pick one from the other. She was high on both, on the call of the moon and the promise of being one with the stranger who'd taken up residence inside her body.

Jay led her to a small copse of trees, so tightly circled that the trunks surrounded them like a curtain. "I'm going to show you how to find your wolf, set her free." He turned her to face him and pulled her close, so close his mouth hovered over hers. She could feel every rapid breath as he exhaled. "How to shift."

She tugged at the top button on his shirt, easing it undone. "First I have to be naked."

A hint of a smile curved the corners of his lips. "Then why are you undressing me?"

Growling, Eden closed her teeth on his lower lip and ripped her own shirt open. Buttons popped off, disappearing beneath the pine needles and fallen leaves, and she let the rent fabric drift to the ground to join them.

Jay cupped her ribcage and brushed his thumb over the lace of her bra. "I like this. It's very pretty, but I'm about to rip it."

"If you don't, I will."

"On second thought..." He slipped his fingers under the strap and tugged it off her shoulder. "That won't help you control your transformation."

The adrenaline boiling through her veins made that clear, but she still felt a stab of disappointment. "Later," she rasped, tugging her jeans open. "The houses will be soundproofed when we get back."

"If Stella's half as good as she says she is." He grasped the tab of her zipper and jerked it down.

Every move was a tease. Foreplay, even with sex as a far distant goal. He was playing with her, stroking desire and taunting her wolf, bringing both to the surface as fear and nerves drifted away. Eden fumbled with her bra and groaned as he knelt and took off her shoes.

He stayed at her feet, staring up at her, as he slid her jeans and panties down her legs at the same time. "You feel it, now get control of it. Wrap around it, Eden, and make it yours."

Her skin tingled. Constricted. Or maybe it hadn't changed, but she was growing. Either way, her body didn't fit anymore. She swayed and caught her balance on Jay's shoulders, and his breath spilled across her bare abdomen.

Hers. The power had to be hers. Clenching her eyes shut, she tried to gain control of the rising power. Her wolf snarled, and the pressure turned to pain. "I can't," she growled, her hands spasming. Her fingers twisted painfully, and she whimpered. "She's stronger than me. She's going to rip me apart."

He rose and pressed his forehead to hers. "Doesn't matter. Don't fight, honey. This is just another part of *you*."

Control her power without fighting the wolf. As if it was that easy, like flexing a muscle she'd never used before. "Can you let me feel it through the bond?"

"I can." Jay released her and stepped back, already unbuttoning his shirt.

If Jay undressing her had been foreplay, Jay undressing himself was out-and-out pornography. Grinding her way to an embarrassingly public orgasm against his thigh suddenly seemed tame. Innocent.

This was dirty promise. Jay bared his body in stages, his hot gaze never leaving her. Broad shoulders. Strong chest with dark hair that her fingers itched to touch. Flexing muscles. Lean waist. And lower...

Human shyness screamed for her to avert her gaze. But Jay kicked his pants away and stood before her, naked and smugly self-assured. Eden had never fully appreciated the seductive lure of a shamelessly aroused man.

She did now.

Jay bent low, the smooth arch of his spine rippling as the bone and muscle beneath began to stretch and reform. He closed his eyes and whispered her name. "Feel it, Eden. The most natural thing in the world."

He began to shift, but instead of pain his features remained relaxed, almost beatific. He was at peace, and that peace flowed through their connection and into her. When he finally stood before her on four paws, that peace melted into sheer exultation.

He tipped back his head and howled.

Eden sank to her knees and reached for him, sliding her shaking fingers through the fur at his neck. "You're beautiful," she whispered, awed.

Somewhere in the woods nearby echoed an answering howl, and Jay butted his head against her side.

Closing her eyes, Eden followed the whispers of peace, searching inside herself for a place that resonated with the same tangle of human and beast. The place where they were joined, where her wolf waited with growing impatience.

She brushed *something*, and heat flooded her limbs. Fire, burning painful enough to drive a cry from her lips. Pain enveloped her, froze the air in her lungs so that she couldn't even whimper, couldn't beg Jay for help because this *hurt*, hurt like she was breaking, broken, splitting out of her skin—

Panic gripped her, and she huffed in oxygen and used it to unleash her terror in a wild scream that echoed off the trees as a howl instead of another human cry.

When she lowered her head, Jay was there, his shoulder against hers. He nudged the side of her muzzle with his nose and backed away, his tail held high.

Muzzle.

She took a tentative step. Her paws slipped on the pine needles, and she thumped to the forest floor in an awkward sprawl of legs. For one disorienting moment, she was trapped, she was Eden in a wolf's body, her senses a jumble of unfamiliar input and mounting panic.

Then she inhaled, dragging in the scent of the woods and the smell of her partner—her mate—and the wolf surged. Pain snapped through her chest, followed by a flood of relief, like a badly set bone had been jerked into alignment. She was no longer human or wolf.

She was human *and* wolf.

Surging to her feet, Eden bounded toward Jay, crashing into his side with a giddy lack of concern. She nipped at his flank and danced away, daring him to follow her, to play with her.

He lunged after her with a soft growl, his jaws closing lightly on her tail. Then he raced past her as a short yap blended with a lower howl to rise in the night—an invitation, one Eden felt in her bones.

She followed him. She couldn't do anything else.

A large, reddish-brown wolf broke free of the trees ahead of them. Power rushed before him, whipping through the trees, a wary, restrained strength that could only belong to Fletcher.

Jay eased between them, his ears straight and his gaze steady. He seemed to be both welcoming and warning Fletcher at the same time, a notion confirmed when he growled with a slight baring of teeth.

Mine. This one is mine.

Yes, that was how it should be.

Fletcher didn't back down, but he did back off, giving Jay and Eden space as more wolves appeared. Their forms were unfamiliar, but Eden felt them with that same newly awakened sense that told her when Lorelei was uneasy or Mae frightened. A taste in the air, an aura she couldn't quite see.

Colin felt strong and a little wild, his danger tempered by the way he fell into place at Jay's side with clear deference. Shane hung back, keeping a bit of distance between them as Lorelei—it *had* to be Lorelei—moved closer to Eden's side, her head held low.

Submissive, but not so much as Mae. Kaley danced around her, encouraging her to play, but Mae crept forward, her ears flat against her head, tail tucked low. She stopped a few feet short of Eden and Jay and rolled to her back, baring her neck and belly.

One by one, they circled and sniffed, stepped into the places they'd spoken of as humans—dominant, subordinate— but speaking had been different. Words compared to these actions, to the way Fletcher and even Kaley moved more carefully than the others. Wary.

Watching.

As humans, they could choose their paths. As wolves, it would always come down to this. Instinct, the gut knowledge of what was right and proper...and what was undeniably wrong.

Eden barely knew them. She barely knew herself. But she knew what she was, here and now. Leader. Protector.

Alpha.

Tilting her head back, she let joy carry her voice, let it lift through the trees and into the bright afternoon sky. A second howl joined hers, lower and rougher, a familiar sound from her childhood. Zack welcomed her to his world with a howl that held everything—affection and gratitude, loss and regret.

And—for one terrifying second—farewell.

The moment slipped away as a third wolf joined, and a fourth. It was beautiful, an eerie harmony that swelled in her heart. A song that promised she'd found the place she belonged. When she launched herself into the trees, carried forward by the lingering music, she didn't worry that she'd find herself running alone.

She'd never be alone again.

Chapter Eleven

Some things never changed, and that included the four of them.

Jay dodged a playful lunge and a nip from Shane and wanted to laugh when Kaley took the other wolf down with a triumphant shove. It came out as a barking yip, a reminder that he'd gone far too long without shedding his skin like this.

He'd changed every month, of course, as most wolves did, but running alone was nothing compared to running with a pack. They'd chased each other as the sun dipped below the horizon, as the sky faded from bright blue to purple and then to an inky darkness that spread out over the woods like a blanket.

Now, Jay had a different chase in mind. The others headed back toward the house, but he urged Eden to the barn instead. His blood pulsed with heat, the kind that would carry over to his human form.

They needed to be alone.

Eden nipped at his flank and charged past him, challenge singing along their bond. She'd found her place in the pack, but her wolf still wanted to be wooed by her mate. Stalked and claimed, won by right of strength.

She ran into the shadows deeper inside the barn, but Jay stopped and knelt. The change flowed through him, harder than before because of the call of the moon...and easier because of what awaited him.

Awaited *them*.

He rasped her name as he rose. He shut the wide door, latched it and turned.

Labored breathing. A whimper. Moonlight spilled through the barn as her magic rose, and she emerged from the shadows as a human, skin and hair equally pale in the silver light.

Not her eyes, though. Her eyes glowed, molten gold and hot enough to set the barn on fire. "Jay."

He took a single step toward her. "Do you want to wait?"

"I don't care if the whole pack lines up to peer through the windows." Her fingers flexed as she took a step toward him, graceful and predatory. "We're not mated. Not truly."

But they would be. The pounding in his blood demanded it, so Jay reached for her, tangling his fingers in her hair. "You won't submit."

"I know," she agreed, dragging her nails down his chest. "And you forgot your handcuffs."

"Another time." He'd have her, he just had to fight for the right to call her his. The possibilities made him even hotter, and he licked a slow path over her jaw.

Her hand reached his hip. She dug in, scratching his skin, and her chest rose and fell with each sharp breath. "I don't know the rules. I don't know how hard I can fight without you giving up. I don't know if it's fucked up that I have to wonder that."

"I won't give up." He murmured the words against her mouth. "Not now, Eden. Not ever."

"Good." Her tongue flicked against his mouth before she bit him, sinking her teeth into his lower lip with a satisfied snarl.

His body reacted with lightning speed, hardening before he could take another breath. He wrenched her head back and hummed against her throat. "You said you wanted to play."

"Is this how we play?" She twisted before he could answer, testing his grip on her hair by trying to lunge away.

He let her go, his hands falling by his sides. "Play. Stalk. Whatever you want to call it."

"Stalk." Her glazed gaze seemed to judge the distance to the opposite side of the barn. Her breasts lifted and fell with her unsteady breaths. "You promised you'd chase me," she whispered, the challenge covering fragile vulnerability. Then she bolted.

Finally.

He caught her by a hay bale piled high with extra items she'd brought from her house, including a stack of threadbare quilts. He locked one arm around her waist and lifted her high, nuzzled the back of her neck through her hair. "Say yes."

"Yes." It came out breathless. Hungry. "Yes, yes, *yes.*"

Jay pulled the top quilt from the bale and unfurled it with a snap of his wrist. It landed askew, lumped up on two corners, but he dragged Eden down to it anyway. "I'll do this in a bed too. Wherever you want."

"Your truck?" She tangled her fingers in his hair and pulled his mouth to her arched neck. "I always wanted to make out with you in your truck."

On a summer night, slick with sweat under their clothes. Jay groaned. "You like that?"

"Mmm." She shivered when he touched her, her entire body seemingly hypersensitive. "Groping. Panting until the windows are all foggy."

"Like teenagers?" He licked her skin, then hovered over the spot where her pulse beat at the base of her throat. "You want me to mark you."

She clenched her hands, tugging at his hair. Pulling him closer. "Like you did the first night."

He'd done it then to satisfy instinct. Now, his hands shook as he pressed his lips to her pulse. "Not exactly like that. More."

"Tell me." She rocked her hips, ground up against him already slick and ready. "Show me."

He caught her wrists, pinned them above her head and bit her—hard. She cried out, back arching, and for one dizzying moment the bond between them slammed open. Eden rushed through it, alive and wild, open to him. Utterly unprotected, utterly vulnerable.

One moment of blind trust. Of sweet, willing submission.

Instinct and blind need demanded that he take her, claim her for his own. Instead, he rubbed his cock against her once, twice. "Again. Let me feel that, all of it."

She moaned. "Maybe I will, if you bite me other places."

"You really want to wait that long right now?" He flexed his hips.

Eden froze, her breath rasping through the darkness. "Condoms. I'm not—do we need condoms? Can werewolves get pregnant?"

The question flustered him. He told himself it was because he should have already thought of it. "Not you. Not yet, I mean—because you're new."

Eden had already moved on. She squirmed beneath him, lifting her hips in impatient demand. "Then take me. *Take* me."

Every movement stroked his cock, wet and even more inviting than her words. Jay let go of her wrists and slipped one hand down under her hips. "Look at me."

Her unfocused gaze slid to his face. "Now, Jay. God, *now*."

He kept his eyes locked on hers as he pushed against her, then closed his eyes with a groan as he thrust inside. Her body clasped his, warm and tight, and his arm trembled as he held himself above her.

Eden lifted her hips to meet him, her pleasure sparking bright across their bond. "I can feel you feeling me. It's...it's..."

"So fucking hot." Obscene, but nothing else described the way they fit together, the arousal already melting into bliss.

She scratched his back, panting as she urged him to rock. "If we come too fast can we do it again?"

All night long, over and over, until the hunger burning inside them both had been sated. Jay held her tight as he pulled away, buried his face in the hollow of her throat and drove into her.

Pleasure. Need. Her fingernails broke the skin on his back. "Harder."

"Not yet. Just like...this." He punctuated the words with another thrust.

She moaned and seized his mouth, licking past his lips to find his tongue as her body trembled beneath him. One more rock of his hips against hers, but it wasn't enough.

It wasn't *enough.*

Jay pulled away, back on his knees, and dragged Eden up against him for a short, blistering kiss. Then he turned her over so she was kneeling on the blanket and leaned over her.

"Yes," she hissed, sliding her hands across the blanket until her back formed a sloping arch. She rested her cheek against her forearm and lifted her hips.

Her skin was soft under his mouth, sweet under his tongue. "Say it."

She bit off a curse and rocked back with an embarrassed noise. "Fuck. Fuck me."

She whispered the words as if she'd never said anything that filthy in her whole life. Jay pushed into her slowly and slipped one hand under her to tease her clit. "Not so shy, honey."

Growling, Eden rolled her hips, grinding against him. "I've thought a lot of dirty words. Saying them out loud is different."

"Saying them is sexy as hell." He stayed still but circled his fingertips over her pussy, not just her clit but the slick inner lips as well.

156

"Jay." She reared up, twisting around to bare her teeth in a snarling challenge. "Are you going to fuck me or not?"

He gripped her hips and drove into her. She flung her head back, mouth wide and eyes squeezed shut. The bond stripped away all her secrets, feeding him the jolt she got from a deep thrust at a sharp angle.

He pushed her upper body closer to the quilt with one hand between her shoulder blades and plunged into her again. Another jolt, even sharper this time, and Jay groaned her name.

"Again." Her body tensed, her fingers gripping the edge of the quilt. "Right there, again, *harder—*"

She'd called it fucking, but the need strung out between them was deeper, unavoidable and undeniable. Mating, pure and simple, the closest either of them could ever be to another.

He rode her harder but no faster, dipping his mouth to the line of her spine. "You're beautiful. You're mine."

No response but a broken cry, and the warmth that flooded him as her body clasped him tighter. "Almost, almos—oh my God."

Her pleasure flowed through him, burning and so far beyond the physical that he barely felt his own body, only hers. He yanked her to his chest and bit her shoulder. "Not done."

Eden twisted her head and caught him on the chin, her teeth scraping possessively over his skin. "Mine."

He shuddered and held her mouth to his jaw. "Harder."

She licked him instead, tongue hot and teasing. "You're hot when you're bossy."

"Bite me again, Eden." He put steel behind the words this time, a command he knew would get a response. "See what it feels like, making me come."

Eden slid her fingers up his arm to where his hand cupped her jaw, holding her in place. Her fingers ghosted over his, then tugged, urging him to curl his hand around the front of her throat. "Not bossy enough," she whispered against his chin before biting him hard enough to bruise.

She wanted to walk the edge. Jay tightened his fingers, just a little, and resumed a grinding rock that had her gasping as she squirmed in his grasp. Her wriggling struggles sharpened her excitement, and a light, teasing graze over her clit was all it took to send her spinning straight off that edge again.

Every pulse of her pleasure echoed through him, setting off shivering heat at the base of his spine. His orgasm built, tense and swift, and exploded with two final hard thrusts.

Eden's head thumped back against his shoulder. She moaned, her throat vibrating against his palm. "Hottest sex ever."

"Shh." He wrapped both arms around her and hid a smile against the back of her shoulder. "I'm enjoying the moment."

"Good moment." She sounded giddy, though she seemed perfectly content to relax back against him.

An old quilt in an even older barn—one hell of a first time. "I probably did this all wrong, but I don't give a damn."

"If this is you doing it wrong, I'm not sure I can handle you doing it right."

"Even if you couldn't...I've got handcuffs, remember?"

She moaned softly as her head fell forward. "Our rooms had better be soundproofed after tonight. I want you to do bad, bad things to me."

Jay rolled to the quilt and pulled her into his arms. "Soon, maybe, we won't have to stay here every night. After this mess with Memphis is sorted out."

"I don't mind it as much as I thought I would." She settled her cheek on his arm with a sigh. "It's been surreal. I took the vacation from work and I've been out here every day, living this new life with these new people. And in two days I have to go back to the library and be...human."

At least, with his job, he had a reasonable excuse to hustle out to the farm if the need arose. "Do you feel steady enough for that?"

"I think so. Besides, I don't have a choice. They weren't happy about my emergency personal vacation."

But they'd be even less happy if she lost her temper in another meeting. "Eden, this is something that happens to new wolves sometimes. They have to change jobs—change lives, even—because nothing fits right anymore. I'm not saying that's you. I'm just saying be careful."

Silence. She traced her fingertips along his palm in an absent caress, but her shoulders tightened. "I don't feel as unsteady anymore. It builds up, but it doesn't hurt like it used to. The bond, I guess, or maybe I really am stronger than I thought."

He dropped a kiss to her temple. "It only gets better from here, I promise."

"Good." She snuggled back against him, and her body fit against his, soft and warm. "Do you think they'll be okay here during the day once we go back to work? Would the wolves from Memphis risk attacking in broad daylight?"

He remembered the look on the de facto leader's face, the desperation to hold that place no matter what it took. "They'd do damn near anything. But there are other strong wolves here, wolves who can fight, and Shane will find a way to send out a distress call. They won't be helpless."

"Good," she repeated. Her fingers continued up his arm, and she turned her head and licked the inside of his forearm. "Tell me about werewolf stamina. Is it impressive?"

That quickly, his body stirred. "Want me to show you?"

He felt her smile against his biceps. "In loving, excruciating detail."

The smooth flare of her hip beckoned. Jay slid his hand slowly down her side to her thigh. "Now that we've taken the edge off?"

She chuckled and stretched, arching her back languidly. "In our defense, we had *days* of foreplay."

"Anticipation," he declared, "is not the same as foreplay."

"Are you sure?" She moved fast, lunging over him to straddle his stomach. Without looking away from his eyes, she reached behind her back and circled his cock with her fingers. "You made me come on the kitchen table, you know."

Direct, powerful. She was a woman comfortable in her own skin, and it made him even harder. "I remember."

She smiled and stroked him lazily. "You want to know a secret?"

He touched her hips lightly. "Tell me."

"I wasn't really *that* embarrassed when Lorelei walked in." Her thumb worked slowly up and down his shaft. "Something broke in me tonight when the wolf took over. Something that needed to break a long time ago."

"You are who you are, honey." He arched up into her touch. "I like it."

She tightened her fingers, turning a light tease into intense friction. "I'm going to learn how to be who I am. I still have to hide from the world, but not from myself anymore. And not you."

"Not me," he agreed. "Eden?"

"Mmm?"

"Don't hold back," he rasped. "Show me who you are."

Bracing her hands on his chest, she lifted her hips and positioned herself over him, her body brushing his cock. "I'm a work in progress."

No, she was perfect, whether she realized it or not. "Practice makes perfect?"

"Does it?" She licked her lips and hovered over him, poised teasingly on the edge. "Fuck me, Jay."

"I did." He splayed a hand across the small of her back and sat up straight. "Your turn."

"No turns." She slid down, taking him deep with a roll of her hips. "Just both fucking. Maybe all the time."

"All the time?" He bent his head and flicked his tongue over her nipple. "I can do that."

Her moan bled into a hungry growl, as if the touch had broken some chain on her self-control. She sank her fingers into his hair and dragged his head back, arched his neck until his pulse beat fast and strong under her mouth. Her breath tickled his skin. Her tongue flicked out. Teased.

"Mine," she whispered, and marked him.

It blazed heat through him, a combination of pain and a warmth that tightened his chest until it ached. *Mine.* A word and more—a promise. A vow.

He gripped her hips again, letting his fingertips bite into her skin. "Yes."

She shuddered and whispered another word, one laced with an edge of the wolf. "Mate."

The second time should have been slower, but the moon was high and hot in their blood. Jay urged her to move, and arched back his head when she circled her hips over his. "Faster."

"Yes," she groaned, and then she *was* fucking him. Fast and wild, skin slicking over his as she rode him, wallowed in him, claimed him and got off on it. She flung her head back and closed her eyes, as lost in him as he'd always wanted to be in her.

Her hair tangled around his fingers as he cupped her shoulders, and he licked the hollow of her throat before sucking the delicate skin between his teeth.

She cried out, and her tempo changed. She rocked her hips, ground down hard, and came with his name on her lips. Jay tightened his teeth, turning the bruise into a bite as her orgasm melted into his, everything shared across their bond— and doubled because of it.

He cradled her, panting against her damp skin. Finally, she sighed softly and dropped her head to his shoulder. "Good stamina," she mumbled, sounding sleepily dazed.

Too fast to burn all the way through her first full moon. Once she'd slept a bit, she'd wake up restless again, ready to run.

And Jay was ready to run beside her.

Chapter Twelve

"Got more pancakes ready?"

Shane slid a few stacks onto the serving plate in Jay's outstretched hand. "We need a bigger griddle, especially for the morning after the full moon."

Jay shrugged and set the plate in the middle of the table. "Add it to the list."

"My dad might have some ideas." Eden snatched a pancake off the top of the stack with a grin. "He said this kitchen hasn't been updated in half a century, so if we're going to do it, we might as well think a little less farmhouse and a little more industrial."

"Which sounds expensive," Jay pointed out. Lord knew they'd have enough to worry about just keeping the place running until some of the business investments they'd planned started to pay off.

"Not necessarily." Lorelei poured herself another cup of coffee. "If Austin has some good contacts, you can get plenty of commercial equipment secondhand. You boys are good enough with your hands to handle most of the basic renovations, which just leaves tricky stuff like electrical and plumbing. Easy to subcontract out."

"I know someone," Eden said. "I had to have the wiring on my house redone a few years ago. He's friends with my father and he'll cut us a deal. Dad feeds him enough free—"

"Shit." Colin turned away from the window, his face grim. "Car coming up the drive. Fast."

For all his warnings to Eden the night before, it didn't seem like the Memphis alphas' style, a head-on attack in broad daylight. Jay would have expected something sneakier. Deadlier. "There could be more coming through the back. Fletcher, go take a look—howl if there's anything going on beyond the barn. Shane, go wake Stella."

The wolves at the breakfast table scattered as if they'd practiced for this moment a hundred times, synchronized in a way they hadn't been before the full moon. Colin fell in on Jay's left as he headed for the front door. Eden followed them as far as the stairs, blocking the only way up to where Kaley and Mae still slept.

The car screeched to a stop, the engine still rumbling, but the wolves in it weren't enforcers. A woman with dark circles under her eyes pulled a little boy from the back seat and clutched him to her chest as three more people spilled out of the car, some beaten. Bloody.

Jay's first thought was of a trap, and he steeled himself against their terrified expressions as he stepped off the porch. "This is private property."

"Sanctuary," the woman whispered, fingers tightening on the boy. "They said this was sanctuary."

Oh, *shit.* "You came from Memphis?"

Lorelei folded her arms across her midsection. "That's Tammy. One of Christian's women."

Agony twisted the woman's features. "We do what we have to when there's no hope. You know that as well as anyone, Lorelei."

"I never gave him anyone else," Lorelei whispered fiercely. "I never set anyone up. I didn't do what you did to Zack!"

The boy made a frightened noise. Tammy slid a protective hand to the back of his head, hiding his face against her neck. "You don't have a son."

Pain flashed across Lorelei's face, harsh and gone in an instant. "How the hell would you know?"

Jay laid a hand on her arm. "Go inside. Ask Eden if she'll get the extra rooms ready."

He could tell she wanted to argue. She even opened her mouth to give voice to the protest sparking in her eyes, but in the end Lorelei turned and walked back into the house.

Jay rubbed his face. "I won't have any trouble here. That's the first and last rule, the only important one. This is a safe place, but only if we keep it that way."

"We couldn't have stopped them." Lorelei's challenge had given the woman spine, but without it she seemed lost. Exhausted. Tears filled her eyes, and she lowered her gaze to Jay's feet. "Everything Christian did to their pack, he did it to us first. By the time they came for Zack's people, most of us just wanted to keep breathing. We don't want trouble. We just want to survive."

"Okay. Shut the car off and come inside."

One of the other wolves, a man with a puffy black eye, spoke up. "It's hotwired. We had to steal it."

One more bit of danger, something else he'd have to cover up. "Shane?" he called.

But he and the witch were already pushing through the screen door. "I heard. I'll take care of it."

Whether the car ended up in a chop shop or at the bottom of a lake, Jay really didn't care. He motioned to the others. "Get your stuff and come inside. Food or rest first?"

"Rest," Tammy whispered. "Thank you. Thank you so much. We won't make trouble, we'll pull our weight. I can work—"

"For now, you can rest," Eden said, stepping out onto the porch next to Jay. "If you come with me to the smaller house, we have an empty room already set up. We may have to do some rearranging, but I think we can get all of you bedded down near each other. Sound good, Jay?" Though she made it sound like a question, she turned her back on the new arrivals long enough to say, "Colin will explain."

He didn't have to. Whether they'd been coerced into it or not, these new arrivals had hurt the others, and everyone would be better off with a little space.

Eden exuded confidence and dominant power as she hopped down the steps. She swept the tired wolves ahead of her, herding them toward the little house as she admired Tammy's son and held out the promise of hot baths and soft beds.

As her voice drifted out of easy hearing range, Colin stepped out onto the creaky porch. "Lorelei's really rattled, and I take it Kaley doesn't need to find out they're here while they're within choking range."

"Not if Peters used any of them to get to Zack," Jay agreed. "You know it might be a trap."

"Might be just as dangerous if it isn't. You think that kid is his?"

"Shit, I don't know. Those are two very bad choices—Trojan horse versus insane asshole bent on reclaiming what's his? I think we're just about out of time, either way."

Colin snarled his agreement. "Eden asked if Shane and I would move over to this house. The girls seemed okay around us last night, and I'd feel better being on hand."

"It's a good move. Fletcher can stay over there, keep an eye on things."

"He'll probably want to." Colin crossed his arms over his chest. "He's trying not to dig in, get too attached."

"I know." Every step closer to belonging was one step closer to an inevitable fight. "He doesn't want this pack, but things are what they are."

"Fletcher doesn't follow," Colin agreed. "Back in the day, I wasn't much for it either."

He said it as though everything had changed. Jay leaned against the porch railing and focused on his friend. "And now?"

Colin closed his eyes. "I've spent ten years hunting monsters. Stalking them. Getting into their heads, figuring out how to take them down. That's too much time thinking like a monster. I don't know if I trust myself anymore."

Too long without boundaries. Orders. "You're welcome to stay, man. As long as you need to."

"I need to stay. I *want* to." He rubbed a hand over his hair. "I'm tired of revenge. I want to protect someone so they don't need avenging."

"That's the goal, right?" Jay held out his hand. "I'm glad you're going to be here, Colin. Damn glad."

"Might be nice to stay in one place for a while." Colin clasped Jay's hand. "We could build something here, once this is over. Something real nice."

A safe place, a haven. "Sanctuary," Jay murmured. It was all any of them wanted.

Eden had been in her office for all of two minutes when a member of the board knocked on the partially open door. Virginia Burke must have been waiting to pounce from the moment Eden set foot in the library, and from the look on the older woman's face, Eden knew she wasn't going to like what was coming.

She set her address book next to the stack of mail she'd been sorting through and fixed a smile on her face. "Come on in, Virginia. It's nice to see you."

"Likewise." Virginia closed the door almost silently behind her. "I've left you several voicemail messages over the last few days."

"I wasn't due back until tomorrow," she reminded Virginia, keeping her voice as light as her smile. Bright and happy, even if the wolf was unamused by this intruder in their territory.

The woman arched an eyebrow. "Yes, I know. I was calling to see if you'd resolved your family emergency."

Eden had known this conversation was coming, but somehow it felt worse sprung on her like this. She wanted to have it on her terms, at her time, not trapped in her office with Virginia's perfume strong enough to give a werewolf a migraine. "Actually, I was hoping to talk to the board. I know everyone's worked hard to give me the time to deal with this, but I might need a few more days. Just to get everything settled."

"More time?" Virginia released a breath on a heavy sigh. "Eden, I know that Albus's boy is back in town. Everyone does."

Zack's absence had put most of the cruel whispers about him to rest, but Eden still remembered being a child. She remembered women like Virginia whispering in church and gossiping at the grocery store, fiercely shocked and secretly delighted by what a bad end that Zack Green would come to.

Temper stirred, a hot pressure beneath her skin. Maybe Jay had been right. Maybe she wasn't ready. She couldn't even sound friendly as she ground out one word. "And?"

Virginia didn't avert her gaze. "I would advise you, as a friend, to distance yourself from his problems as much as possible. Come back to work, Eden. Whatever trouble he's gotten himself into, whatever path he's taken, you can't help him. Only the Lord can do that."

Eden fisted her hands. If she gripped the edge of the desk in her current mood, she'd snap the thing in half. "I wasn't raised to turn my back on family," she said, spacing each word out to be slow and clear. "If you have a problem with my work performance or my need for time off, then I'll be happy to discuss it."

"I understand." Virginia took a step back. "I'll have to take your request for extended leave to the board."

They'd expect her back at work tomorrow. Memphis could have attacked by then, or there could be another crisis at the farm. More refugees, more people needing help. Every moment she spent away from Green Pines felt like a moment waiting to hear something had gone wrong. Waiting for the other shoe to drop, just like she had her whole life.

And now she'd be waiting to get fired. It would happen. Standing in her mundane, paper-cluttered office, Eden could see the truth with cruel starkness. She didn't fit in this tiny room anymore. It had been her sanctuary, her cocoon, but now the only thing she liked about it was remembering Jay on the fire escape, luring her out for a kiss.

They have to change jobs—change lives, even—because nothing fits right anymore.

God damn it, she was tired of waiting for things to happen to her.

Moving carefully, she picked up her address book and her mail. "I think I can save the board some time. Considering the likelihood that family obligations will be taking up an increasing amount of my attention, it would probably be smart to offer you my resignation."

Virginia started. "Eden, you should think about this. Don't be hasty."

"If you need me to help with the transition, I'll do everything I can." Eden dumped her address book in her purse and tossed her organizer in after it. "I'm sorry, Virginia."

"I don't even..." The woman held up her hands. "Write it up, and I'll take it to the board. But Eden—be careful, sweetheart."

Virginia was watching her like she'd lost her mind. None of them had ever seen her make a hasty decision in her careful, claustrophobic life. "I'll be fine," Eden promised, and she meant it. For the first time in years, she could breathe deeply. "Don't worry about me."

"How could I not? What will you *do*? There isn't exactly an abundance of jobs like this in Clover."

Might as well plant the seeds now. People were undoubtedly already whispering about what was going on at Green Pines. "The family that came to stay on the farm has a business selling organic soaps and bath products. They're doing so well, they're expanding their operation. I might help."

Again, that look like she'd gone insane, simply waltzed up to the deep end and jumped off. As if nothing about her made sense anymore.

It was probably an expression Eden would need to get used to.

Chapter Thirteen

"Am I crazy, Dad?"

Her father grimaced and dropped a dollop of whipped cream on top of her slice of apple pie. "You're not crazy. You're going through some stuff, and you've got to find your feet again, that's all. If you start listening to Ginny Burke—*that's* when I'll know you've lost your marbles, kiddo."

"If you say so." It was her second slice of apple pie—and if being able to metabolize it quickly wasn't a fringe benefit of being a werewolf, she didn't know what was—but she thought her father's approval had done more to soothe her doubts than his baking. "She's right about one thing, though. I can't keep the house without a job unless I dip into my savings, and I don't want to do that if I don't have to."

"I can help you out with that," he assured her.

"No, Dad. You've got the diner to worry about already. And you've always helped out with taxes on the farm."

"Well, you have to have someplace to *live*, Edie."

She dragged her fork through the whipped cream, leaving little indentions behind. "I was thinking..."

He bent far enough to catch her gaze. "Of what?"

"Moving back to the farm." She didn't add *with Jay*. Not that they'd discussed as much, but after last night she was having a hard time imagining a bed of hers that didn't have him in it.

Which wasn't something she planned to admit to her father.

But he only nodded. "Last I checked, Chief Ancheta was spending most of his time out there too."

Eden avoided his gaze again and cursed herself for blushing. "Most of his time, yeah. Probably less once he has to go back to work."

"Maybe," he agreed. "I'm glad, you know. That there's something going on out there at the farm now that doesn't have anything to do with bad memories. It's a good thing, a nice change."

She thought about the shadows. The whispers and chills, the breezes that tickled the back of the neck and vanished. "Sometimes I still think it's haunted," she admitted. "I never really grew out of seeing ghosts out there, I guess."

Her father gave her a stern look. "It's not haunted, sweetheart. It's just...a sad place."

"I guess." She took a forkful of pie and let the sweetness distract her from how little she wanted to ask her next question. "Has Zack been talking to you? I barely see him."

"He's stopped by a few times." Austin started wiping the counter. "He talks a little, tells me stories about Lorelei and Mae. Sometimes he wants to talk about the folks who didn't make it."

At least he'd been confiding in someone. It eased a pressure in her chest she hadn't realized was there. "They lost a lot of people. It'll take some time for everyone to heal, but they're starting to get there."

Her father stilled and lowered his voice. "You never said how things went. The full moon?"

She couldn't describe it in words. Fear melting into joy. Strangers becoming family. "It was good. I'm good." She put down the fork and reached across the counter to grab his hand. "I'm great. I really am."

"You promise?"

"Absolutely."

A slow smile spread over his face, bringing out the deep-set wrinkles around his mouth and eyes. "You don't know how glad I am to hear that, Edie."

Lifting up, she leaned over to kiss his cheek. "I know you've worried about me. But I feel like things are falling into place."

"As long as you're happy, that's all I need." A bit of his smile faded. "You haven't always felt like you belonged, knowing what you did about Zack and his mother. A whole other world that wasn't part of everyone else's. I'm sorry we didn't handle that better, your mom and me."

Eden settled back down on her stool. "You did your best. That's all any of us do. I just wish..."

He tensed. "Wish what?"

He probably already knew. She'd been a child—a scared, awkward child—how well could she have hidden it? But in all the years since, they'd never discussed it. The secret was a splinter, one that had festered for years.

"I wish I'd told you," she whispered. No one was close enough to hear, but it was easier to say if the words were nothing but soft breath. "Zack made me promise not to tell anyone how bad it was, but I wish I had. Maybe I wouldn't still wonder if I could have made it better."

His hands tightened around the towel. "We didn't know how bad it was. If we had, it wouldn't have mattered—" He looked up, his gaze clashing with Eden's. "Your mom and I talked about taking Zack, it must have been a hundred times. There were reasons we didn't—why we *couldn't*—but none of it was ever your fault. Not ever."

"I know." She covered her father's hands with her own. They felt fragile now, old and worn and human, and she had so much more strength at her disposal. "I'm still working on believing it in my gut, but that's another thing that takes time."

He stared at her in silence for long moments, not even breathing, and finally sighed. "Time. It's supposed to heal all."

Was he thinking of Zack's childhood, or the more recent loss of her mother? "Does it?"

The last customer of the lunch rush called out a farewell and pushed through the door, leaving them alone. Austin set aside the dishtowel and braced his hands on the counter. "Your mother didn't know. She wouldn't have understood, and that's not an excuse. It's the truth, and I...didn't want to lose her."

A shiver of warning shook Eden as she studied her father, his tense shoulders and racing heart.

Fear. "What didn't she know, Dad?"

He didn't seem to hear her. "When I would talk about Zack, how he needed to come live with us, Albus would threaten me. Said he'd tell Marla everything, and my happy little family wouldn't be so happy anymore. And I knew he was right, damn it, because Kathy was the one thing your mother didn't understand."

Kathy. Zack's mother. "I thought she was gone before you met Mom."

"Before we were together, yes. But your mother knew her. She knew—" His voice broke. "I loved her."

"Oh." Oh, *God.* So much pain in his face, in his eyes, and Eden was afraid to ask the question hanging between them. "I—I didn't realize."

He rounded the counter and dropped to the stool beside hers. "You weren't meant to, Edie. No one was. Kathy... I don't think she loved me. She was lonely, God knows—Albus treated her like shit—but that's all. A stupid kid and his brother's lonesome wife. A bad country song, that's what it was." His eyes clouded. "Except for Zack."

Zack, who looked more like her father than she did. Looked more like her father than he had Albus. Oh, she'd heard the rumors, the spiteful whispers. She'd discounted them the same way she'd ignored everything else the small-town rumor mill spit out about Zack—because they didn't know what she did. They didn't know who he was, *what* he was.

She shook her head, denying the words her father hadn't said. "His father was another werewolf. That's why he was born a wolf."

"That's what Kathy always said, but it's the only thing that makes sense. The only reason for the resemblance—and I know you see it. Just about everyone in this damn town has."

If Albus had confirmed the town's suspicions, no force on earth could have convinced them it wasn't true. *But he's a werewolf* wasn't a workable defense in the court of public opinion.

And why was she thinking about that when Zack could be—

Oh, God. "You think he's my brother."

"It's supposed to be impossible," he said. "But maybe it was meant to be, that magic, one-in-a-million chance...and I blew it. I left him alone to deal with a man who beat the hell out of him."

Numb shock held most of her frozen. All except the quiet, analytical part of her brain, which drew a careful line between a baby who shouldn't have been born a wolf and a woman who shouldn't have changed before the full moon. Two data points were barely a coincidence. They weren't a pattern.

Except if one was possible... "I wasn't supposed to change when I did," she heard herself whispering, the confession tumbling free without her permission. She wanted to yank the words back, to bite her tongue and tell her father that everything was okay, that he hadn't abandoned his son out of fear.

But the words kept coming. "I wasn't supposed to change before the full moon, but I did. Jay and his friends are trying not to freak me out about it, but I know I'm unusual. Maybe the rules aren't as unbreakable as the wolves think."

"Could be." Her father wrapped one arm around her shoulders. "I wanted to tell you. I should have already, just like I should have told Zack. He might want to find out for certain. Then again, he might wish I'd kept my mouth shut. Either way, it's time this family was done with secrets."

Zack had been her big brother in the ways that mattered, acknowledged or not. Knowing shouldn't change anything. But that wasn't how knowing worked.

Knowing always changed everything.

A wave of stress and worry hit Jay first, just before Eden came into the dining room and dropped an open cardboard box onto the trestle table.

"You okay?" he asked, sliding his paperwork over to give her more room.

"Fine." It came out terse and rough, and she gripped the box hard enough to bend it before sighing. "No, not fine. It's been a weird day."

Bothered, but not scared. Jay frowned. "What happened?"

"Before or after I quit my job?"

"You what?" He reached for her hand. "Eden, did something happen?"

"No, no." She twined her fingers with his and circled the table to lean against his shoulder. "That was the good thing. I was standing there in my office and all I wanted to be was back here getting stuff done. Dealing with the new refugees and helping Mae and Kaley get the barn set up. So I made my choice."

She sounded relieved—about that much, at least. "So if you're not upset about your job, what's wrong?"

Her fingers tightened around his hand. "Were any of you born wolves? It seems like everyone I meet was turned, not born."

"Keith, the enforcer from Red Rock. He was born a wolf. Can't really think of anyone else you might have met besides Zack." He tipped his head back to look at her. "It's not as common as it used to be, but it happens."

"Only wolves having babies with other wolves?"

A question as puzzling as her confusion. "Yeah, it has to be two werewolves. I thought you knew that."

She wasn't looking at him. "And wolves never change for the first time before the full moon, either. Except me."

An exception, one that even Stella admitted could have any number of explanations they'd never know. "The kid thing is a little different. Wolves have one first change, but most of them have lots of sex. Babies with humans always turn out human."

Eden tugged her hand free and turned to rummage in the box, surfacing with a meticulously cared-for picture frame. Inside, behind squeaky-clean glass, stood a man and a woman outside Olsen's Diner.

The smiling woman cradled a baby in her arms, and she looked so much like Eden that Jay lingered over the image. When he finally looked at the man, Austin Green's wide, ever-present grin was unmistakable. "Your parents."

"Just over thirty years ago." Her finger hovered over her father's head. "He doesn't look like anyone to you?"

The man looked a little bit like Eden, but mostly he looked like himself—strong jaw and a straight nose, and tall, commanding if not for the humor sparkling in his blue eyes. Then again, if you disregarded the look on the man's face, there *was* something oddly familiar, something Jay had never seen in Austin. A tilt of the head, a particular stance.

"He looks—" He broke off and met Eden's gaze, certain he had to be wrong.

Silently, she pulled another picture out of the box. A birthday party, cake and all, tiny little Eden wearing a sweet smile and Zack, clean-shaven, a broad grin on his face.

Jay's breath caught. "Jesus Christ," he murmured. "Is he your brother?"

"You said he can't be," Eden said just as softly. "But my dad thinks he is."

"DNA testing. Find out for sure." He set both frames on the table. "Does Zack know?"

"I don't know. I don't know anything past what my father told me. That he had an affair with Zack's mom, and my uncle always suspected it."

Staring at the photos, only one question would come. "Why didn't Austin just take Zack?"

"He wanted to." She wrapped her arms around her body and shook her head. "I think Albus threatened to tell my mother everything."

"So?"

Eden's shoulders tensed. "It wasn't a good decision, but he was scared of losing my mother. You know how this town is."

A flimsy excuse. "Maybe, but was your mom the kind of person who would rather have seen a child suffer than find out about her husband's indiscretions?"

"They weren't indiscretions! My parents weren't even married yet—" Her teeth snapped together and she dragged in a breath. "I don't know all the reasons, but my dad cared about Zack. If there'd been a way, he would have taken it. You're the one who said we couldn't have done anything even if we told the law."

The police wouldn't have been able to help...but they wouldn't have *had* to. "I said they couldn't prove abuse. That wouldn't have mattered if Austin had filed for custody as Zack's real father."

That stopped her for a moment, but a prickle of uneasy power accompanied her defensive stance. "Could he have gotten it?"

"It depends, I guess, on the availability of paternity tests. DNA, that sort of thing." He nodded to the frames. "Are you going to tell Zack?"

"Tell Zack what?" Zack cut in, stepping into the doorway.

Eden fell silent, both of her hands closing over the frames as if to hide the pictures. She was frozen, still, as her fear and uncertainty washed through Jay.

He did the only thing he could think of. He deflected. "How to lay tile. Once we get through redoing the kitchen, I think maybe the bathrooms should be next."

"DNA testing and tiling." Zack's flat gaze rested on Jay for a moment before switching to Eden. "I thought you were going back to work today."

"Tomorrow," she managed hoarsely. "But I don't think I'm going back."

"Not going back." The words were so cold, so *empty*.

Every instinct screamed, and Jay suppressed a shudder as he rose and carefully insinuated himself between Eden and Zack. "She quit. To spend more time here at the farm."

"Quit or got fired?"

"Quit," Eden all but snarled. Her temper was rising too, but Jay could sense the panic underneath it. "I quit, Zack. My choice."

"Bullshit. Look me in the eye and tell me those bitches who run the place didn't tell you to stay away from me."

Eden's silence echoed through the room, stricken and helpless.

Jay kept his gaze on Zack. "She's needed here, and that's okay. She's *okay*."

"She's losing her life!" Zack slammed his fist onto the table, his growl eclipsed by the thunderous crack of the wood splitting. Eden's box pitched to the floor, spilling framed pictures and knick-knacks across the floor in a cacophony of shattering glass.

"Zack, *stop*." Jay infused the word with as much alpha power as he could muster.

Zack drove his boot into a piece of the broken table. It skittered across the floor and slammed into the wall, rattling the window in its frame. A sick growl wrenched free of his throat, one of rage and betrayal. "You were supposed to keep her safe."

"I'm okay—" Eden's voice cracked, and he flinched like she'd struck him. His gaze dropped to the shattered table and the broken glass, and he shuddered before spinning out of the room.

Eden started after him, but Jay caught her arm. "Don't. It'll just make it worse, seeing you hurting."

She winced as her shoe crunched on a piece of glass. "I didn't think it would upset him this much. But he blames himself..."

Christ, he didn't want to have this conversation with her. Not ever, but especially not now. "He might not ever stop blaming himself, Eden. I've seen it before. The trauma, the outbursts—it's bad for anyone, but worse for wolves."

Every muscle in her body turned to steel. She knew the truth—on some level she knew it, the instinctive level that had embraced her wolf so completely—but she wouldn't admit it.

"Maybe after the situation with Memphis is settled for good. We're all stressed about it."

Jay had to look away. "Ignoring this won't make it go away. We have to *talk* about it, figure it out."

"If it doesn't get better, then we get him help. He's my family. He could be my *brother.*"

He grasped her arms. "I'm not talking about Zack being depressed or punching a table, Eden. I'm talking about him breaking down, losing control of everything, including the wolf."

She blinked at him, those big eyes impossible to read now. "How do we fix it? Is there magic, or a spell?"

"No, honey. There's nothing like that."

Denial bled into anger. "And what does that mean? You just give up on him?"

"It's not about giving up. It's about protecting the rest of the pack, and protecting him from shit I know he wouldn't want to do if he had any will or sense left."

She didn't look away from him. "Say it, Jay. Say the words."

Her fury burned in his gut, and Jay had to fight not to let it spark his own. "I don't want to. I don't *want* to consider this at all, but I don't have a choice. Zack asked me to take over this pack, and this is part of it. The hard part."

Eden jerked her arms free of his grip, but she didn't back off. "Say the words. If we're going to fight, let's fight for the right reason."

Damn it all. "If he has to be put down," he said quietly, "then I'll do it myself. Quick and painless, I swear."

"Put. Down." She wreathed every word in ice. "You want me to get a DNA test to find out if he's my brother before you kill him."

"I don't want to do anything," he shot back. "Eden, you quit your job and he broke a fucking table. How far from the edge do you think he is?"

"I don't know where the edge *is*! Is it that quick a jump from breaking a table by mistake to having to die?"

Zack had been born a wolf, lived with that superhuman strength all his life. Nothing he broke could be by *mistake*. But in her position, Jay would probably have to turn it around too, if only because the knowledge was terrifying, and accepting it unthinkable.

He took a deep breath. "I didn't say that, and it's not about the table. You know it isn't."

"I know. It's about what we have to do, and what we can live with." Pain twisted her features, a sad echo of the agony trembling across their bond. But even now he could feel her pulling away. Fighting to put up walls, to block him from her heart. "I can't stand by and let you kill him. I can't live with that."

The new distance between them hurt, but Jay hid it behind the blankest mask he could manage. "It isn't a subjective matter, Eden. Zack has been putting as much space between him and the rest of us as possible, but it's not enough. If he keeps on the way he has been, at some point, he'll become too dangerous."

"Then I'll find a way to stop it." She turned her back on him and tipped the box upright, as if the conversation was over. "I'll have the dining table from my house brought over tomorrow."

"Eden, don't."

"Don't what? Make plans to fix the things that are broken?"

"No, you—" *Don't push so hard you push him away. Don't blame yourself if you can't change things. Don't get hurt.* "Nothing. You do what you have to do."

She picked up a framed photograph of her and her father standing with Zack at his graduation and shook the broken glass free. It bounced on the floor with a sad clink. "I'm not a helpless little girl anymore. I'm not going to let him get hurt this time."

And the demons plaguing Zack were the same plus some, death and destruction and the kind of failure Eden could only now begin to suspect existed. "Let me help you."

"You can get the broom," she said, her voice devoid of any emotion. Flat and careful, as smooth a mask as her face. She was good at pretending.

"Damn it, I'm not talking about the glass." But she'd already placed the broken frame in the box and started for the door. Jay raised his voice. "Just stop for a second and listen."

She hesitated in the doorway. "I don't know if I can take many more words right now. I've made a lot of hasty decisions today already."

Take your own advice, dumbass. Don't push. "All right. Okay."

Tears brightened her eyes, but she didn't ask for comfort. She turned her back on him and walked away.

Her sadness lingered longer than her anger, and it wrapped around him as he grabbed the broom and began to sweep the glass from the floor. He could have waited, hidden the truth from her. Pretended Zack was fine, that Jay had never seen the flashes of desperation in his eyes, never listened to his pleas for mercy and offered his promise to handle things.

In the end, Jay didn't have to pull the trigger. It was the sort of work Colin had taken upon himself so many times before, eliminating threats with brutal efficiency. Except it was killing him, bit by bit, and having him take on what was rightly *Jay's* responsibility could only push him farther down the path to losing his soul, and maybe even his mind.

No. Eventually, Jay would have had to stand before Eden and have this same conversation. Better now than later. Now, when the cut could be quick and clean.

Mostly.

Chapter Fourteen

Stupid, stupid, stupid, stupid.

The word pulsed with every step she took, a self-loathing refrain pounding in her head. Unshed tears stung her eyes and formed a lump in her throat. She took the long way around the house because she didn't know what to do when she reached the barn. She'd left half of the contents of her box strewn across the dining room floor for Jay to sweep up, and if that didn't feel like a metaphor for her life right now...

One morning. That was all she'd gotten. One morning of bliss, one morning of freedom, feeling comfortable in her skin and so confident of her place. She'd wanted to believe she'd turned a corner in her life. That this new Eden was the *real* Eden, awake and unfettered after so many years of making herself small and numb.

Maybe it had all been a haze of adrenaline and good sex, and she'd thrown over her life in the reckless pursuit of something that could only exist a few hours at a time. And that was the *good* possibility.

The truth burned in her gut like she'd swallowed a hot coal. Zack wasn't right. At some point during the full moon, she'd slid into the wolf and the wolf had slid into her. She knew things now. She *felt* them, knowledge that lived in her cells as if she'd been born with it.

Zack wasn't right. Wasn't just wounded. He was sick, darkness eating him up from the inside out, and Eden hated Jay for saying the words and hated herself more for knowing they were true.

Not that agreeing with him could change anything. If he put down her cousin—her *brother*—how could the human parts of her live with him? How could she live with herself, and the parts of her that would undoubtedly approve? She'd be torn down the middle, mired in self-loathing and addicted to the man who'd ripped her in two.

She stopped at the corner of the house and stared at the barn. She'd pushed Jay last night. Scratched at him, challenged him, skated along the line between violence and sex because there had been something thrilling in the game. Something necessary to satisfy her baser needs.

Such a delicate balance, and it could go so horrifyingly wrong. What would it take to push them off that edge, to stumble over the line from sweet games of power to the sort of nightmare Kathy and Albus had lived out on this farm? Violence and passion, rage and lust.

Maybe it could never happen. Maybe it would only take one step.

Shivering, Eden hurried past the porch and strode toward the barn. Neither of them would take that step. She'd give him up before she became her uncle. Cut out her own heart if she had to. Cut out his too. Better numb and alone than destroying each other and everyone around—

"I don't *want* you to fight. I want you safe. I fucking need you safe. When you say this shit, you're not making it better. You're giving me one more reason to get the hell away from you."

It was Zack's voice, drifting from around the edge of the barn, and Eden froze as Kaley answered.

"Is that what I'm supposed to do? Go away, just not too far?"

Eden could hear the tears in the girl's voice. Her already battered heart broke in half as Zack whispered Kaley's name, full of pain and regret, and Eden *had* to move, because she couldn't listen to any more of this and couldn't let Zack say the words he wouldn't be able to take back.

"No," Kaley continued. "At some point, I'll have to leave. I won't be able to—"

Eden reached the edge of the barn, and Kaley's words cut off in a gasp. When she stepped around in sight of them, Kaley drew away and turned, folding her arms around her body, and Zack jerked around, his eyes going wide. "Eden."

"Sorry," she said, forcing her voice to sound casual. "I was bringing this stuff out to the barn to sort through later and I heard voices."

"I was going for a run anyway." Kaley kicked off her shoes and picked them up. "I'll be back late."

"Don't go too far," Eden warned her. "Jay doesn't want any of us running on our own after dark right now. If you want a long run, you could see if Colin or Shane wants to go."

"Fine," she muttered, already brushing past Eden. "Whatever."

Eden fought a flinch and turned back to Zack. "I'm sorry."

He laughed, strangled and hoarse. "Christ."

"I didn't hear very much." Enough to know he'd probably hope she hadn't heard more. "Are you all right?"

"I screwed everything up," he said calmly. "For them, and now for you too."

The calm was almost as chilling as the outburst in the dining room. "You haven't screwed anything up, Zack. Even if you could take it all back... God, I hate everything that brought you here, but I *like* being a wolf. I like how I feel now."

He nodded, his gaze fixed on a point past her shoulder.

"Zack. Look at me."

He did, but his eyes didn't focus. He was looking at her, but he didn't *see* her. "If I hit a skid, Jay knows what to do. I took care of that already."

Her heart froze. "Don't say that. Jay is the only thing—" The lump was back. She had to squeeze the words out past it. "I think I love him, Zack. If you hadn't come back, I never would have known. And if he has to—it won't matter."

He snapped into focus then. "Yes, it will. Damn it, Eden, don't toss him over stupid shit like that."

"*Stupid shit?*" Her temper slipped as she slammed the box to the ground. "You don't get to tell me your life is stupid shit. You may not value it, but you have to deal with the fact that the rest of us do."

Zack swallowed a growl. "Why would—"

The earth shook. Eden's stomach dropped out, through her feet and into the earth, taking her equilibrium with it. For a moment, she felt like the ground was sucking everything out of her—oxygen, balance, the ability to think. She blinked at Zack, but all she could make out was a blur of him pressing a hand to his head.

It hit her a moment later. Screaming, a warning that rang not across the still night but inside her head.

"Magic," Zack muttered. "Fuck. Did Stella set up something, an early-warning spell in case someone shows up?"

"I don't know." Eden's human mind was still rattled, but the wolf rose to steady her as she turned and started for the house. "We need to find out."

By the time she made it to the front of the house, Jay and Stella were out in the yard. Fletcher stood on the porch at the little house, ushering the latest refugees from Memphis out the door.

"Eden!" Jay's hands fell on her shoulders, heavy and reassuring. "I think it's time. Someone's coming."

188

"Lots of someones." Stella closed her eyes, swayed, then dropped to her knees and reached for a twig. "Clear some space." She began to sketch something into the dirt.

A rough form took shape, a box followed by a single line that curved a meandering path. The shape nagged at Eden, something familiar. Something she'd seen before. "Are you—?"

"Yes." Stella quickly scratched in two boxes, one smaller than the other. Their relative placement and sizes jarred Eden into realization—the farm.

Shane bounded down the porch steps, a bag clutched in one hand. "Is this it?"

The witch closed her eyes again. "Sprinkle it on." He did, and she began to chant. As they watched, two glowing pulses of light swirled up out of the soil, one at the top of the crude map, near the road, and the other at the back edge of the property, through the trees. "Incoming."

Fear settled in her gut, but it was the feral, vicious anticipation that left Eden shivering. "So we need to—"

"She's not here." Zack's hoarse mutter cut through Eden's words, and her breath caught as she searched the wolves gathered around them and realized one was missing.

Only one.

Zack had done the same math. His gaze fell to the ground, where the crude map showed its damning pulse in the woods. He whispered Kaley's name and bolted for the back of the house, even as Eden lunged after him. "*Zack!*"

Jay caught her shirt. "Don't. He'll find her, but we need you here."

You don't care if he lives or dies. She bit down on the words because she knew they were unfair. Zack was the one who didn't care if he lived or died. Jay could have told her as much, but he'd taken that responsibility on himself too.

He'd been a good alpha, and he was demanding the same of her. She stopped trying to jerk away and twisted around far enough to watch Fletcher steady Tammy, who was sheet-pale and clutching at her sobbing child. Mae looked just as bleak, huddling in on herself inside another sweatshirt so huge it had to be Shane's. Even Lorelei was scared.

Kaley could take care of herself, and Zack would shake the world to pieces to protect her, suicidal tendencies or no. Eden choked back her worry and focused on her duty.

Her pack. "Where do you want us to go?"

"Get them in the house. Upstairs." His jaw clenched. "If any of them get past us, it's up to you, Eden."

Yes yes yes, chanted the wolf, trembling with the need to snap the leash and savage the enemies who had harmed her people. She pressed close to Jay, lowering her voice to a whisper. "How? Will I know?"

"Let her out." He dragged her mouth to his, lifting her off her feet for a quick, bruising kiss. "It'll be over soon."

So much left unsaid between them, bad words and good, but they were out of time. She was still trying to form a sentence when he set her on the ground again, and then it really was too late. Jay started barking orders, sending Fletcher and the one able fighter among the new refugees in search of Zack and Kaley in the woods, and it was up to Eden to gather up those too weak to fight.

But not alone. She turned and found that Lorelei had already shaken off her fear and put aside her distaste for the newest refugees. She herded Mae and Tammy toward the front porch as Eden gathered the rest of the new arrivals, soothing them with a rush of power that tasted as much of Jay as it did of her. His strength, always at her disposal through their bond—and shared without reservation.

If—*when*—they got through this, she'd give him all the words she'd held back out of fear. For now, all she could do was feel it, feel it hard enough to sing across their bond and seep into his bones, and maybe give him a different sort of strength.

I believe in you. I want you. I need you. I love you. Come back to me.

Waiting was torture.

Jay clenched his fists and rocked back on his heels, waiting for the first sounds to prick at his ears. They'd have left their vehicles at the road, slipped through the trees lining the long, twisting drive. As little warning as possible, no time for anyone on the farm to prepare before the fight was upon them.

Christian Peters had underestimated them. Again.

Stella brushed one heavy, beaded lock of hair from her face and rose. "Should we go find them?"

"No." Jay growled at the thought. "We stay here and guard the house. They'll come to us. They're being careful, that's all. Don't want us to know they're here, not just yet."

Colin stripped off his shirt, letting the fabric fall carelessly to the dirt beside Stella's sketched map. "What sort of combat magic have you got, and how do I stay out of its way?"

She flexed her fingers as her hand began to glow. "Just don't try to eat me or anyone I like."

His boots and belt joined his shirt before he looked at Jay. "I'm gonna end up trying to tear those bastards' throats out with my teeth either way. Might as well use my sharper teeth."

It would always play out that way, no matter how the fight started. Jay would use his guns until he ran out of ammunition—or until the wolf took over, demanding a chance to bite and rend.

To win.

Shane had already shed his clothes as well by the time the first strange wolf burst out of the thick trees lining the driveway. Jay drew his pistol and fired. The shot winged the creature's shoulder but, more than that, it heralded the pack's readiness to meet the attack.

Another shot, and the wolf fell. Jay fought to still his finger as it itched to pull the trigger, again and again.

A second wolf, then a third and a fourth. Stella muttered a curse and began to chant, and Jay spoke, his voice miraculously even. "Fletcher and the others will work their fight our way. So we hold our ground, and we show these bastards what happens when they violate our sanctuary."

Colin answered with a snarl and lunged toward the wolf on the far right. He was bigger and faster, but it wasn't strength that gave him the advantage. Protective fury seethed in every line of him as he crashed into the first enemy and bore him to the ground, jaw snapping shut on his enemy's shoulder.

Wolves were still spilling from the trees. Six, ten—a dozen. Jay pulled his second pistol and emptied them both. They'd be useless in a close fight anyway, the kind that was coming. Twelve—no, fifteen. Fifteen to four.

Not a fair fight at all. He grinned, more feral snarl than anything, then tossed both handguns aside and yanked at his shirt. "Cover me, Stella."

The witch hit her knees, heedless of the fanged, four-legged creatures bounding toward them. One deep breath, and bits of light began to glow in the air around her, like fireflies converging on her hands. When she slammed her palms to the ground with a shouted word, the earth shook beneath them.

Jay expected to fall, but as he tossed his pants aside, he realized his footing stayed true despite the quaking. Only their attackers pitched and rolled, hit the grass with yelps and whines.

"Magic," he muttered, and dropped to the lawn to call his own, the change that splintered through him like lightning, riding adrenaline and anger.

The strongest of the attackers regained their feet and refocused their line of attack, charging toward Stella with a desperation that stank of fear. Colin, silent and lethal, slammed into them from the side, tumbling one wolf into two of his brothers. He vanished just as quickly, flowing over the ground to guard their right flank.

Shane fought naked, ready to change but still in his human form. When a wolf sprang at him, he caught it in an iron grip, clutched its muzzle and jerked its head around with a lethal crack.

Jay brought down another of the Memphis wolves with a quick snap on a hind leg as it rushed by. The animal tumbled to the grass, biting and snarling, but it was no match for Jay's strength. He dispatched the wolf as pressure built in the air around them, a sensation he already recognized as the prelude to magic.

Stella chanted, her head bowed as Shane ran interference in front of her, holding off attackers. When she lifted her head and opened eyes gone completely white, Jay howled a warning to Colin, who bounded out of the way just in time to avoid the sweeping of her arm.

The pressure exploded outward, and four of the wolves who'd managed to coordinate an attack *detonated*, just blew the hell up in a rain of blood, bone and fur.

Jesus Christ. Jay took a hard blow to his left flank as the interlopers scrambled to reform, attack harder or faster, but Colin and Jay and Shane and Stella met every advance head-on, and with brutal efficiency.

Something was wrong. The wolves fought with purpose, but no clear leader. No direction, no rallying howls of encouragement.

Christian Peters wasn't among them.

Jay feinted right to avoid a desperate attack and pulled up short when another wolf charged, knocking him over. Beyond the house and the barn, the sounds of a second fight drifted closer. Maybe Peters was with the other group, cowardly enough to sneak in the back way while most of his pack fighters died in the front yard.

It wouldn't do him any good.

Chapter Fifteen

Tammy's son couldn't stop crying.

Silent tears. They tracked down his pale face as he huddled small and terrified in his mother's arms, and even though his too-thin shoulders shook with each sob, he didn't make a noise. He cried like someone who knew how to make himself invisible, like someone used to hiding from the monsters.

Eden didn't know how to soothe him when his own mother's whispers didn't help, when the walls weren't thick enough to hide the sound of battle. It surrounded the house now, which was why they'd crowded into the empty bedroom at the top of the stairs. One window, one door, no balcony.

No *space*. It wasn't a large room, and agitated werewolves seemed to take up more than just physical space. Tammy and her son were tucked in the corner with the two weaker males from Memphis. Mae leaned against the wall with her eyes closed, drawing in breaths too slow and uniform to be anything but a conscious effort to stay calm.

Eden stood next to Lorelei and lowered her voice, though Mae would be able to hear a whisper. "Is she going to be okay?"

Lorelei watched the door. "When it's over. She'll be fine when it's over."

"Soon," Eden promised, though it felt like a lie. So many howls. Could Jay keep them all from breaking through their lines? Even if fighting that many wasn't impossible, keeping track of them might be.

It would only take one. Shivering, Eden bent to remove her shoes and socks. Better to be ready, which meant stripping naked so she could change at a moment's notice.

She had her shirt off and was reaching for the hooks on her bra when something thumped lightly in the hallway. "Lorelei, get back in the corner with the others."

"I don't think so." She stood beside Eden, her hands at her sides. "You need a beta, right?"

Someone who could stand at her side, the way Colin stood next to Jay. Eden grabbed Lorelei's hand and squeezed it once. "I need you to keep the others out of my way. If someone comes through that door, I'm giving in to the wolf. And I don't know if she'll know how to stop fighting once she starts."

"No one else is running into this fight," Lorelei murmured. "No one else could. Just you."

Footsteps whispered on the other side of the door. Eden released Lorelei, inhaled deeply and caught the scent of wolf and something sharp, almost metallic. No, not a scent, a taste— like chewing tin foil. It raised the hair on her arms and curled her lips back into a snarl as the doorknob twisted slowly.

In the corner, Tammy whimpered, high and terrified, and Eden *knew* who was coming for them, even if she didn't recognize the tall, coolly handsome man who pushed open the door.

Lorelei snatched a pistol out of the back of her waistband. "Get out, Christian. *Now.*"

Talking, not shooting. If Eden were any good with firearms, she'd have snatched the thing out of Lorelei's grasp and shot the bastard herself, but distraction now could prove fatal. "Shoot him," she whispered, dragging power up from the depths of her being.

Christian laughed. "Shoot me? Lorelei doesn't shoot people. Lorelei rolls over like a good bitch and does whatever it takes to keep a man distracted. Don't you, pretty pet?"

Her jaw clenched, and she gripped the butt of the gun so hard her knuckles turned white. "I'll find a way to do it this time," she whispered. "For them." Her thumb eased the safety button off with an audible click.

Christian laughed again, a sound full of grating disdain riding dominant power. It shredded through Lorelei and smashed into Eden, and for the first time she recognized the true difference between them. Lorelei swayed as if the power had snuffed out her will.

Eden felt nothing but rage. Clean, sweet fury.

The gun slipped from Lorelei's limp fingers, and Eden caught it in midair. Time constricted as the wolf flooded her, turning an awkward grasp into a smooth spin. *Grab the gun. Push Lorelei back toward the others.* Eden swooped up to face Christian as she squeezed the trigger.

Unfortunately, she wasn't the only one who was fast. Her two bullets sank into the doorframe as Christian disappeared into the hallway. She lunged after him, still firing, aware of only one thing. She had to drive him away from her people, away from trembling Lorelei and terrified Mae and Tammy's little boy, who had seen so many monsters already.

Silence in the hallway, not even footsteps. And then Christian's voice rang out from nowhere. "You might as well put it down, sweetheart."

Eden edged into the doorway and peeked in both directions. The short hallway leading to the front bedrooms stood empty, all of the doors still shut. To the right, the craft and sitting room was a cluttered mess, stuffed with Mae's sewing and stacks of unpacked boxes, but no wolf. Not unless he was hunched in the blind corner opposite the sliding door.

Lifting the gun, she took one careful step forward. "I won't have any problem shooting you."

"Won't you?"

The disembodied whisper shivered past her. Eden spun toward the front of the house again, but no one was there.

The metallic taste had returned, sharp and bitter in her mouth. Magic. "You're such a fucking coward you need to hide from a bunch of women and a crying kid?" she demanded, straining to listen for the reply. It *had* to have a direction.

A low, husky laugh. "Do those mind games work on the shitheads around here?"

She swung in the direction of the sound and fired, but the bullet dug uselessly into the far wall. "I'm not the one playing hide and seek."

"No." A door slammed across the hall—Zack's door. "How many bullets will that little gun hold? How many have you fired?"

Eden groped behind her for the doorknob and hauled the door shut behind her. With her back against the solid wood, Christian couldn't get into the room without going through her.

She almost hoped he'd try. Right now she thought she could gladly rip out his throat without shifting forms first. "Almost enough bullets to bring backup. Want me to fire a few more out the window to bring the men running?"

"You could try." A force slammed into her hand, knocking the gun free. It landed with a thump and skittered down the hall.

Human instinct screamed for her to lunge after it. Her muscles tensed in anticipation of a move, but her wolf flowed up and snatched control, flooding her with steely resolve.

The weakest members of her pack were behind the door at her back. She wasn't budging until the threat against them was dying or already dead.

Human sight was only a distraction. She closed her eyes and reached out with that part of her that could slide down the bond connecting her to Jay. He'd closed his emotions off from her, undoubtedly to keep her from worrying, but she wasn't grasping for him. She was reaching out, out, out, feeling beyond herself with a new awareness.

Instinct.

She felt Lorelei. Mae. The shattered pieces of a woman that must be Tammy, and the terror of her son. Two males, tired and hopeless, reeking of defeat and resigned to death.

And metal. Stinging cold and deadly. Not a wolf—a spell meant to hide one. It flowed toward her in a rush, and she jerked aside just before a force crashed into the door directly where her head had been.

Eden flung her hand toward the sick pulse of magic and closed her fingers around empty air. Except it wasn't empty—it was a tangible force that singed her palm, a warning jolt that raised every hair on her body as if lightning was about to obliterate her. Screaming her defiance, she tightened her grip and jerked hard, tearing the spell from its anchor.

The wooden disc burned in her hand, and Christian Peters appeared in front of her, his mouth already curling into a sneer.

Then he punched her in the face. It knocked her wits sideways, and that was his fatal mistake.

Eden's mind skittered in a thousand panicked directions, and instinct took over. Her wolf knew nothing about fighting in human skin, but she knew plenty about vulnerable spots and pressing an advantage.

An opponent who laughed smugly instead of swinging again was an advantage. While Christian was still congratulating himself for planting his fist in Eden's face, she whipped around, caught him by the shirt and slammed him face first into the wall with all the werewolf strength she still couldn't control.

He didn't make that mistake again. He shook off the blow with a growl and kicked at her knee. Fast, but not faster than her. She wrenched to the side and lunged past him, raking her fingers down his face. She left bloody furrows in her wake, marks that would sting but not slow him down.

That was all right. Hurt his body, sting his pride. Awkward and ineffective fighting was a trap that could lure him away from the people she needed to protect. She backed down the hall and scrambled for the gun. He'd have to follow her, if only to keep her from shooting him in the back.

His hand slammed into her shoulder, and she pitched forward into the wall. Christian loomed over her, snarling, and grabbed her by the hair. The movement lifted his arm, and she drove her elbow back into his ribs hard enough to crack bone. His fingers tightened reflexively, ripping at her hair, but she ignored the pain. Instead, she used those scant seconds to tear free of his grip with so much pain she wondered faintly how much of her scalp she'd left behind.

Footsteps sounded too loudly behind her, Christian already recovered and advancing again. She crashed into the table where Mae did her sewing and, whispering a silent apology, snatched up the fancy new sewing machine and whirled, swinging it at his injured side.

Too slow. He slid to the side and the machine crashed through the sliding glass door and slammed against the porch railing.

"That wasn't smart." He locked his arm around her throat and squeezed—hard.

She fought to twist away, but he had almost as much werewolf strength and *far* more human bulk. This time he was braced against her elbows. Trying to kick him only resulted in him hefting his arm up until her toes barely dragged against the ground.

No air. She couldn't draw in breath, and werewolves needed it. They must need it. If she rolled her eyes to the right, she could see the door to Quinn's room. The memory of his body flashed through her mind unbidden, dangling from a rope, discolored and lifeless—

No. Eden groped for the table again, fingers scrambling over fabric and fringed tassels—the curtains Mae had been sewing. Then her fingertips brushed something hard.

With the edges of the room already graying in her vision, she fumbled the curtains aside and closed her hand around the long metal fabric scissors. She remembered purchasing them with Fletcher's money, remembered him urging her to get the large expensive set that would *last* instead of something cheap and plastic.

God bless him.

Gripping the handle, she whipped the pointy end of those massive, shiny shears around to sink into Christian's gut.

He screamed, a sound full of as much rage as pain, and footsteps thundered down the hall. Lorelei and Mae, though it was hard to make out their faces with the room swimming. Mae turned toward the head of the stairs but stopped and threw open the second-floor window with a cry for help.

Eden ignored them both and stabbed Christian again. The scissors grew slick with blood, and she shifted her grip, weaving her fingers through the handhold as she sank the blades deep and twisted until he dropped her.

Air rushed into her lungs, sparking pain and a dizzy sense of giddiness. She wanted to bend over and gasp in deep breaths until she was drunk on oxygen, but the wolf wouldn't rest with an unfallen adversary behind her. Spinning around, she met

Christian's dark, shocked gaze and sank the blood-slicked scissors into his throat.

She followed him down, and she didn't let go until Lorelei covered her bloodied hands and tugged. "He's dead, Eden. Gone."

Christian was still under her. Silent. His blood covered Eden's body, soaked through her bra and jeans and slicked over her skin. So much blood, and he wasn't bleeding anymore. He was dead. Not breathing, not moving, not bleeding *dead*.

She still couldn't ease her grip on the scissors. "Are they fighting in the front yard? Can you see through the window?"

"They're coming in," Mae called down the hallway, even as footsteps pounded up the stairs.

Jay stumbled onto the top landing, his bare feet sliding in the blood that slicked the floor. His throat worked, and he gripped the edge of the open doorway, his voice low and full of dread. "Eden—"

She found every mark on him. Scratches that were all but healed, deeper wounds that knit together even as she watched. She cataloged them because it was the only thing she could do, because her fingers still weren't unclenching and God, he was *alive*. "I can't let go."

He was by her side in an instant, his body wrapped half around hers even as he knelt beside her. "It's okay." He closed his hand around hers and pressed his lips to her temple. "Just breathe."

Breathing brought the sharp scent of blood, metallic and overwhelming. Eden squeezed her eyes shut and fought to block out everything but his touch. "I'm okay. I promise. I'm just..."

Jay trembled. "How the hell did he get in here?"

"He had a—a thing..."

"A charm," Mae supplied, holding up a bit of leather strung through a wooden disc.

"A charm." Taking in another slow breath, Eden released the scissors and turned her hand palm up. Under the blood, just below her middle finger, an angry burn mark marred her skin. "I couldn't see him, but I could feel the magic."

Jay hissed in a breath, his questing fingers hovering just over her palm. "Fletcher and Colin are handling things outside. Mae, go tell Stella to make a sweep, check for more magic like that." He touched Eden's hand finally, a light brush across her wrist. "Let's get you cleaned up, okay?"

Looking down was a mistake. She was straddling Christian, her knees in a pool of blood that seemed to go on for miles. It covered everything, soaking into her jeans, clinging to her bare skin, covering her in tangible proof of what she'd done.

Easy to say she wanted to rip the bastard's throat out. Facing the gruesome, bloody truth of it—

She jerked her gaze away and found Lorelei hovering there, eyes worried, ready to step forward and help. Ready to take care of Eden.

She shouldn't have to, and that stiffened Eden's spine just enough. Somehow she kept her voice even as she let Jay help her to her feet. "Can you go check on Tammy and the others? And close the door. I don't want her son to see me when we walk by."

"Don't worry about that right now." He slipped his arm around her waist, supporting her when her knees might have buckled.

Worrying about it was silly, but it kept her together as Jay half-carried her down the hallway and into the upstairs bathroom. Mae and Kaley's soap and toiletries cluttered half of the double sink, with only Zack's razor and toothbrush as proof he existed at all.

"Zack," she whispered, stumbling toward the tub. "Are Zack and Kaley all right?"

"Fletcher found them." Jay turned her around and tugged at the hooks fastening her bra. "They had to fight a handful of the Memphis wolves, but they made out okay."

He peeled the sticky fabric from her chest, and Eden shuddered and closed her eyes. "I need to learn how to fight. Teach me. Promise."

"We all need to learn a lot of things." He unbuttoned her jeans. "I'll get the water running."

He bent toward the faucet as she struggled with her jeans, shoving the fabric down her legs in jerky stages, as if she could only concentrate on one tiny task at a time. Details. Little details, like the bite mark on Jay's shoulder, or the linoleum peeling up in the corner, or the way her zipper felt cold under her feet when she stumbled free. If she focused on the details, then the world didn't have to be real.

Jay's quiet voice broke through the haze. "I'm sorry I didn't—that I wasn't in here with you."

"No. No, Jay..." The numbness shattered when she touched him, and she clung to his shoulders and buried her face against his throat. "I can be strong for them, as long as I get to be freaked out with you."

He locked his arms around her waist as steam began to billow up around them. "I knew this wouldn't be an easy fight. I never wanted you to have to deal with this, but not because I thought you couldn't. I didn't have any doubts about that."

Truth. It had a scent, a feeling, like the words took up more space. They echoed in her bones and she turned her ear to his chest, savoring the strong, steady beat of his heart. With him she was utterly safe, and no one should have to wait until they were thirty-two to know how that felt.

Her father had tried, but he'd made mistakes. The only way to be whole was to admit it. "I'm sorry I got defensive about my dad and Zack. I think I'm afraid to be mad at them."

"No, hey. Come on." He lifted her into the shower and climbed in after her. His hands moved with an efficiency that spoke of experience, of the fact that this was far from the first time he'd washed blood from flesh. "You don't need to be thinking about that right now."

"I do." She tilted her head back and wiped beads of water from his cheeks. "I lie to myself about how I grew up. I pretend none of it hurt me because I wasn't as bad off as Zack, and I tell myself my dad was great because he wasn't Albus. I couldn't let myself get angry about it, because it wouldn't be fair to people like you and Zack, people who were *hurt* by their parents. Really, actually hurt."

Jay stroked some of the tangles from her hair. "There's more than one way to be hurt, Eden. And hurting for someone else can be just as bad."

"I need to stop lying to myself." Her tears mingled with the water, but it wouldn't matter. She didn't need to hide. "It makes me weak. Just promise you'll be patient while I learn how."

He tilted her head under the spray and soaped her hair before answering quietly, "It gets easier."

It had to. The first step into truth was the scariest, plunging blindly off the ledge into free fall. But Jay would cushion her landing. And if it hurt too much, he'd help her put herself back together, just like he was doing now.

His hands were soothing as they smoothed away all external evidence of the fight. Eventually, the water swirling down the drain faded from red to pink. When it ran clear, they stood there under the spray, wrapped around one another. Eden pressed her lips to the healing scratch on Jay's shoulder as the hot water pounded the tension from her shoulders, and wished the moment could last forever.

But it couldn't. Too soon, the door rattled under a quick, efficient knock. "We need you guys outside," Colin said, his tone almost apologetic. "Zack's freaking out. I'm leaving clothes outside the door for you."

Jay tensed and leaned out of the shower to snatch a towel from the rack beside the sink. "What's wrong with him?"

"He says there's a body missing. He's trying to get Stella to cast more spells, find the one who's left. Fletcher thinks one of you will have to talk him down."

Eden switched off the water and steeled her shoulders. "We'll be right there."

Jay handed her a second towel as he retrieved the clothes. "Maybe he doesn't know that Peters came in the house."

"Maybe," she agreed, but as dried off and pulled on her clothing, she couldn't help the growing dread. It seemed like years had passed since their fight in the dining room, but the words were barely cold.

The alphas from Memphis were only the outward danger. Zack was still losing his mind, and Jay would still have to deal with it.

Colin had said Zack was freaking out.

Colin had a talent for understatement.

Jay edged in front of Eden as he pushed through the back door, where Zack circled the yard, dragging each dead wolf up by the scruff of the neck and inhaling sharply.

Sniffing. "I know what the fucker looks like," he snarled as he tossed a savaged white wolf aside with no regard for the blood left on his hands. "I'm telling you, he's *not here*."

The beads woven into Stella's hair clicked as she shook her head. "And *I* told *you*, I believe you. But there's no one else here, man. I got nada."

Jay stepped between them. "Who's missing?"

He might as well have remained silent. "Do it again," Zack demanded, jabbing a finger at Stella. "Cast your spell again. He'd be here."

"Who?" Jay asked again, louder this time.

"The fucking bastard brother!" Zack roared, lifting another dead enemy. He sniffed again and growled. "Where the fuck is he?"

"He isn't here," Kaley said, her voice thick with tears. "You've looked at all the bodies twice already, Zack. Jonas isn't—"

He just growled and went to the next wolf. "Cast the spell, witch."

Stella bristled. "Hey, I have a name."

Jay pulled her aside. "Peters had a charm on him, something that masked his presence with magic. Can you take a look at it, see if you can get a feel for what kind of spell it used? Just in case."

She relented with a shrug. "Yeah, sure. I'll get on it."

Zack stalked toward another wolf. Eden cast Jay a worried look and moved to intercept him. "Zack, hold on a second. Let Stella try her spell."

He bared his teeth at her, this growl rising up from deep in his chest. He looked through Eden like he barely saw her, his words short and chopped. "Out of my way."

Someone had to stop this before it spiraled out of control. Jay called on every ounce of alpha power he possessed before easing between Zack and Eden. "Calm down." He lowered his voice. "You're scaring the others."

"Then they can be scared," he muttered, gaze flicking to the side. It fixed on empty space for just a moment before he shoved past Jay. "Gotta find Jonas."

Jay held up both hands. "Wait *one* minute, Zack, and let Stella do her thing."

Zack jerked to the side, shoved both hands into his hair and paced back toward the first wolf. "He has to be here. He *has* to be. It isn't over until he's dead."

"We'll find him," Jay murmured. "And then it'll be over. I promise."

The words skated right past Zack. He rolled the first wolf over with his boot and crouched down. "Must've missed something," he muttered, staring at his blood-streaked fingers. "He wasn't in the pieces. I looked."

Urgency was understandable, but Zack's obsessive insistence chilled Jay's blood. "He may not be here at all. He may be back in Memphis. Hell, Peters might have killed him already for something we don't even know about."

A shudder rolled through Zack. "No. *No.* I have to finish it tonight, or I won't—" He shot to his feet. "Where the hell is the damn spell?"

"It's done." Stella held up the charm Eden had snatched off Christian Peters. "There's nothing with this signature anywhere around here. There's just *nothing.*"

"Fuck." He kicked the limp wolf aside and lunged to the next one, the one he'd been sniffing when Jay walked outside. Each movement seemed increasingly frantic as Zack ran his hands over reddened fur. "Gotta be here. Gotta be done. *Tonight*, damn it..."

A pained noise escaped Eden as she tangled her fingers in Jay's shirt. "Zack, he's one man. Stella's wards will warn us if he comes here—"

"No!" Zack stumbled to his feet and whirled. "I can't wait for him."

Demanding an explanation felt like intrusion, as if it would only agitate the man further, but Jay knew with sudden certainty that the answer mattered. The answer was everything. "But *why?*"

"Because *he's here!*" Zack raised his voice. "I know you are, motherfucker. Show your cowardly ass so I can tear out your throat. You can die like your brother did."

Jay kept his tone level, calm. The way he dealt with violent drunks and crazy bastards. "He's not, Zack. There's no one else."

Zack jabbed a finger at him. "I'll prove you wrong. I'll fucking find him if I have to turn over every rock and tear up every tree on this property."

"No."

Zack jerked to a halt, outrage and disbelief distorting his face into a furious, feral parody of the man he was. "No? *No?* Who the fuck do you think you are? This is *my* home, *my* land."

The others had begun to gather as Jay and Zack faced off. The confrontation drew them in spite of their better judgment, instinct trumping courtesy, though everyone kept a safe distance.

Everyone but Kaley, who finally broke her stillness as Zack vibrated with barely leashed anger. She reached for him, laid a hand on his arm, and he whipped around with a startled roar, striking out with his balled fist.

The blow caught her with enough force to snap her head hard to the left. Hard enough to kill a human, maybe, because even Kaley reeled and went down on her knees in the grass. Lorelei dove after her with a startled cry, already lifting the girl's battered face to the moonlight by the time the realization of what he'd done washed over Zack's features.

Eden shoved past Jay and skidded to the ground next to Kaley. Zack stumbled back, shaking his head faster and faster as one word fell from his lips in a silent chant that grew to a crescendo, a shrieked denial. "No, no, no. *No!*"

Something close to chaos erupted, with people crowding around Kaley, muttering or even crying. Under the din, another noise drew Jay's attention, a sound that had him moving before he realized what was happening. The soft scratch of metal against rough fabric, a rustling whisper that equaled death.

He'd barely crossed half the space between them when Zack lifted the pistol he'd drawn to his own temple, his finger tight on the trigger. Jay hit him hard, bearing him to the ground, and the shot went wide as more screams erupted in the night.

The gun skittered across the grass, and Zack writhed under him, clawing after it. "Do it, Ancheta. Fucking do it, or let me."

"No. I changed my mind." He pulled Zack's arm up behind him and pinned it there to still the man's squirming. "I thought maybe you were too far gone. I even tried to prepare Eden for what we might have to do if you really lost it. But tonight? Fuck that, Zack. You're still kicking, you still care, and you're going to fight, damn it."

Zack shuddered. "Caring isn't enough. I'm hurting people. My people—*your* people. Protect them from me."

Kaley started to sob, a sound even more heartbreaking because one glance told Jay she wasn't crying out of physical pain or even fear. Her gaze was fixed on the gun, terrified and angry, as if it were a living, evil thing instead of a tool.

"I am protecting them," Jay answered. "From losing you. It's the only thing they can't survive right now."

The fight went out of Zack, from Jay's words or Kaley's sobs or simple exhaustion. He rested his forehead on the grass and whispered one final plea. "Keep me away from her."

"Get off of him." The words, calm but tremulous, came from Austin, who stood near the corner of the house, a shotgun in his hands. "People in town were talking about some kind of ruckus out here, so I figured I'd come see if there was fighting to be done. Looks like it's over now."

"Dad—" Eden's voice broke. "Dad, it's complicated."

"Seems so," he agreed. "Are you all right, Edie?"

"I'm fine. We're all going to be okay. Right, Zack?"

A helpless, breathless laugh wheezed out of Zack as he turned his head to glare up at Jay. "You're not going to let me tell her no, are you?"

As if not letting someone blow their brains out on your watch was tantamount to dictating their every word. Jay snarled as he rose. "Get up, Green."

Zack made it to his knees before his gaze fell on the knot of people surrounding Kaley. Agony contorted his features, and he closed his eyes. "Is she—"

"Uh-uh." Jay shook his head. "You want out of here that badly?"

"Not want. Need."

It took a damn twisted sort of situation for a man to need escape from his friends and loved ones so badly. It took something far worse for a wolf to abandon his pack. "Austin?"

"Yeah?" The man's eyes were guarded as he faced Jay.

He *had* to say it, even if it hurt, because Zack was part of his pack, no matter how much he needed time away. "Eden told me everything—about Kathy, about Zack. And about you." Jay squared his shoulders. "One day, you and I, we're going to have it out over what you left your boy to deal with. But not tonight."

Austin swallowed hard, tears welling. "I reckon that's better than I deserve." He handed his gun off to Shane, brushed some grass from the front of Zack's shirt and grasped his shoulders. "Chief Ancheta, it's about time I took my son home."

Eden rose with a soft noise and started toward them, trailing to a stop when Zack closed his eyes and shook his head. "You don't need to do this, Austin," he whispered. "It's not—you don't know that it's true, that it's even possible. And I'm a fucking mess."

"Maybe, but you're *my* fucking mess. I love you, and I've learned you don't walk away from that, kid."

"Go with him." Eden circled her father to bracket Zack, standing at his left as Jay stood on his right. "If we need another fighter, you can be here plenty fast. And if we don't, you can rest. Let him help you, Zack. He's pretty good at the dad thing."

"I can't steal your damn dad."

"It's not stealing," she snapped back, the words edged in a steely growl. "I've wanted to share him with you pretty much all my life. So wipe off your hands, thank him for the invitation and put your ass in his truck. *Now.*"

Zack opened his eyes and stared at Austin. "She sounds like her mother."

"Her mother was a smart lady."

"All right. I'll go. But I need to go now. I can't—I can't do goodbyes."

Eden shook her head. "It's not goodbye. You'll be a few miles down the road, not across the world. Go home with Dad, get some rest, and I'll talk to you tomorrow, okay?"

He mumbled something bordering on assent and started for the driveway, stopping when he drew even with Kaley. "I'm sorry," he whispered, soft words that carried through the night silence all too easily. "I'm so, so—"

"Don't," she cut in. "You didn't mean to do that. Don't leave because of it."

"That's exactly why I need to leave, Kaley. I get confused, I get wound up, and I do things I don't mean to do." His eyes were bleak. Tired. "You won't be so quick to forgive next time if Mae's the one I didn't mean to hit."

Her gaze flicked again to the fallen gun nestled in the grass. "You're not going to end up like Quinn. Remember that you promised."

"I promise." He turned his back on her—turned his back on all of them.

Jay slipped his arm around Eden's shoulders as her father and her brother walked away, out of sight around the front of the house. In the wild, an injured wolf might slink off alone to lick his wounds. Zack could do that, after a fashion, but with the support of his family and friends. Time—and space—to do a little healing. And then...

He could start over.

Chapter Sixteen

Eden spent most of the day unpacking boxes and setting up the master bedroom in the big house, but it didn't feel like home until Jay walked through the door, dragging a suitcase of his own.

It had been hard, sending him back to work when she had to face the morning after with a wounded, broken-hearted pack. But Lorelei had rallied in the way only she could, and Eden could do no less in the face of such stubborn strength. They'd attacked the problem of moving Eden's things together, and the onerous task of unpacking and organizing became less tedious as others drifted in to help them.

Pack building a den together. Family building a home together.

Home, but incomplete without her mate. He looked handsome in his uniform, and felt even better when she stepped close enough to wallow in the power he exuded as naturally as breathing. "I missed you."

"Good, because I missed you too." He slipped an arm around her waist. "How'd it go today?"

"We got through. Kaley may need a bit of space, but as long as we keep an eye on her..." Eden rested her forehead on Jay's shoulder and sighed. "Did you stop by the diner on your way home?"

"I did. Your dad says hi, and to tell you that Zack's going to be okay, so stop worrying."

She choked on a laugh. "I'm that predictable, huh?"

He smiled against her temple. "Anyone in your position would be right now. That's your family."

"Some of my family," she corrected softly. She eased back and circled around him, sliding the door shut with a soft *click* and the gentle buzz of wards humming to life. Stella's clever soundproofing, which would let them steal rare snatches of privacy in the midst of chaos. "Pack's family too."

"Yes, it is." Jay tensed, more a feeling that echoed across their bond than a physical reaction. "I'm sorry, honey. I shouldn't have hit you with that stuff about Zack last night."

Eden pressed her forehead to the door, because it was easier to have this discussion with her back to him. "You had to. I think I wouldn't have gotten so angry if it hadn't felt...true. If the wolf hadn't been so loud inside me, telling me you were right. I couldn't listen."

"And no wonder. I didn't have to be wrong to be a jackass."

"Fine. You were right *and* a jackass." Turning, she smiled wanly at him. "I need time, Jay. I'm glad I have this viciousness when bad guys are trying to choke me. But I can't be glad that some part of me can look at my cousin—my *brother*—and make a cold assessment that he's too dangerous. I'm not ready to be that pragmatic."

He brushed his thumb over the corner of her mouth. "You don't have to be. He was there, Eden, at the edge, and his mind is still his own. He'll make it."

"You made him fight. Thank you." She turned her face into his hand, pressed a kiss to his palm and savored the spark that zipped through her. They'd had a lifetime worth of courtship and responsibility shoehorned into so few days, it was hard to remember that touching him was so new.

"You're welcome."

Smiling, she nuzzled his wrist. "Do you hear that?"

He grinned. "Hear what?"

"Exactly. Everyone's already relaxing in their soundproofed rooms. Nothing's on fire. No one's attacking. No panic, no emergencies...just you and me and a few minutes to breathe."

Jay laughed. "Says you. Work was a madhouse today."

"That's what happens when the chief takes a week off." She traced her fingers along his belt before tugging his polo shirt free of his pants. "Anything you couldn't handle?"

"Just catch-up crap." He caught one of the belt loops on her jeans and pulled her closer. "What about you? Thinking about talking to the committee about your job?"

"Not even a little. I'm going to try being a stay-at-home alpha for a little while." The skin of his back heated under her touch, as if the sparks stirring desire to life burned in him, too. She smoothed her hands around his waist and up his chest, then pushed him back with a teasing smile.

Making him fight for her wasn't getting old, it turned out. Not that he couldn't tease back. He tilted his head and casually pulled his shirt over his head.

The sight of him wasn't getting old either. Eden leaned back against the door and took her time admiring him. For the first time, it felt like...every other encounter had been shrouded in anxiety or fear or the pulsing adrenaline of the full moon.

Tonight he was a man. Her man. And she could trace the way his muscles moved gracefully under his skin all night, if she wanted. "I love you."

She hadn't meant to say the words. For a moment she froze, petrified that it was too much, too fast, but he braced his hands on the door and leaned over her, his forehead to hers.

For a long moment, he simply stood there. Then, "I love you too, honey. I have...for a while."

Eden closed her eyes and floated on relief. "So I wasn't the only one with a secret crush?"

"Not even close." He leaned in farther and kissed her lightly, but light wasn't enough. Eden tilted her head and licked his lips with a hungry growl before burying her hands in his hair. Nothing could ever be enough. Not kissing him forever, not holding him forever, not loving him forever.

Wouldn't stop her from trying. She dug her teeth into his lower lip. "Can we ravish each other now?"

He swallowed a groan. "Do we have enough time for a proper ravishing?"

"This may be our only chance, Chief Ancheta. You going to waste it?"

"Nope." Hunger echoed through the bond between them as he locked an arm around her waist, lifted her and dropped her on top of the blessedly bare dresser. "I know better."

"Good." She sank her fingers into his hair again and dragged her nails across his scalp teasingly. "What's involved in a proper ravishing? It can't be handcuffs, since I see you've forgotten them again."

"Time," he declared, the words muffled as his lips met her throat. "And effort. Mostly the effort. With a dash of creativity."

She'd never been this impatient with any other man. Or maybe she'd simply never been this impatient as a woman. She was more now, a woman and a wolf, an alpha burning for her mate, and Jay's soft, slow touches stoked arousal and frustration in equal measure.

Foreplay took too long, the wolf decided, and Eden had torn open her shirt before the thought finished. She grabbed at Jay's belt with a growl. "Less time, more effort."

He caught her hands and twisted them behind her back. "You can't choose one over the other, or it isn't a proper ravishing."

"Oh." Jerking at his grip did nothing. He had all the leverage and she didn't *really* want to escape, but trying still got her hot and bothered. "So educate me," she whispered. Challenged. "Show me how you ravish your mate."

He kissed her, slow and wet, his tongue following the line of her lower lip. It was raw, unchecked lust, and she shuddered under the assault and pressed her lips together, fighting the natural urge to open to him.

His laugh blew hot on her mouth, but instead of becoming more insistent, his caresses gentled. Slowed.

It only stoked her hunger. Her pulse throbbed throughout her entire body, pooling need between her thighs and setting her nipples to aching. She arched her back, struggling to reach him, to rub against him. Jay relaxed his hold enough to let her, and growled when she pressed her breasts to his chest.

"Too much clothing," she whispered, coaxing. He still had her hands trapped, and his fingers tightened when she tried to move. "Bra's in the way. I want your skin against mine."

He released her, ran his fingers up under her shirt to unhook her bra. "Take it all off, then put your hands back where they were."

She slid her half-ruined shirt down to pool on the dresser and took her time with the bra, wallowing in his hungry expression as she peeled the fabric from her skin. "You want my hands somewhere, you better put them there. Because I'm going for your belt again if you don't stop me."

"Impatient," he rumbled, pushing her wrists back to pin them at the small of her back. "Leave them there."

Eden laughed and bit his chin. "And you thought I was joking about the handcuffs. Better invest in a spare pair, because I think I like misbehaving."

"You could misbehave," he agreed. "Go for my belt. Go *wild*, Eden. But then you'll never know what I plan to do next."

Oh yeah, he knew how to tame her. Not brute strength, but clever words. Whispers that stirred curiosity to life, and even the wolf could be patient for a little while. Her next nip was playful, teeth scraping along his jaw before she licked him, nuzzled into his chin in a brief moment of quiet submission.

"That's right." He combed his fingers through her hair, tugging just enough to tingle anticipation up her spine. "Remember..." He opened her pants and pushed them down, easing them under and off her body. "Hands behind your back."

She twisted her fingers together as a desperate reminder, all too aware of how the posture thrust her breasts out. There was something dirty about being naked while he wasn't, something that should feel vulnerable but was instead empowering. She felt it in the way his breath hitched when she arched her back, and the jump in his pulse when she eased her knees apart.

Desire. Lust. And a look in his dark eyes that eclipsed both. Eden wet her lips and tilted her head back, leaving her throat as exposed as the rest of her body. "Show me what comes next."

Jay held her gaze as he leaned down and licked the spot between her breasts. Good, but not enough. She whimpered and twisted, keeping her hands tucked at the small of her back but urging him toward her nipple. "Please?"

He hummed and touched just the tip of his tongue to her nipple, a warm caress that vanished as quickly as it had come.

Patience cracked around the edges, and her next plea came out riding a growl. "*Jay.*"

His mouth closed around the tight peak, hot and wet, and he sucked hard for only a moment before dropping to his knees in front of the dresser and pushing her thighs even wider.

Staring down at him, Eden stopped moving. She stopped breathing. Everything inside her coiled tight, tensed against his first touch. She had just enough air in her lungs to whisper his name.

He murmured hers back at her, then rubbed his fingers through her folds. Pleasure jolted all the way down to her toes, and she thumped her head against the wall with a moan. "Don't tease. I want you too much."

"I know." His thumb slicked over her clit, followed a mere moment later by the wet rasp of his tongue.

Heaven.

She fell into it, closing her eyes as the world narrowed to his mouth and how very, very clever he was with it. Languid pleasure tightened with urgency, and she didn't remember moving her hands, just sliding them into his hair with a greedy noise she couldn't help. "More, God, just like that."

"Mmm." A hard thrust, his fingers sliding inside her, and she clung to him as her body jerked, a response beyond her control when he went straight for the spot that pulsed through her like lightning. Instinct had her wiggling back, clinging to the scraps of her control.

He licked her again, slowly, and curled his fingers inside her in a gentle rocking motion.

No mercy. No respite, just the slow unraveling of anything human until she was a creature of hunger and impulse, writhing as he brought her up and up and up, so high, so *good*—

"Let me come," she begged, tugging at his hair. "Make me come."

And then he did, but not in a relieving rush. He thrust her over the edge and let her fall, let her crash into shaking spasms that had barely subsided before his fingers crooked. She opened her mouth to protest, to beg for a moment to collect herself, but his tongue found her clit again, rasping, demanding, and the growl that vibrated against her rocketed her back to the sharp, oh-so-sweet edge.

He held her there. He held her there until she was twisting and begging, and this time when he pushed her over, he didn't let her fall. He caught her halfway down, as her voice broke on a helpless cry, and dragged her back to her peak. Release crashed into wanting melted into coming twisted into needing, and somewhere in the foggy distance, the remains of her ecstasy-splintered mind recognized that *this* must be what it was like to fuck a determined man who could feel everything he did to your body. Who could track every reaction, time every touch...

And then even those scraps of thought shattered into nothingness as he drove her up one last time only to sweep her over the edge into limb-melting release.

Jay tangled his fingers in her hair and whispered against her cheek as she floated down, her ears ringing. And when she finally opened her eyes, he nipped her lower lip. *"That's* how you ravish your mate."

"Wow." Eden tilted her head enough to rub her cheek against his. "And you're still wearing pants. Damn."

"Mm-hmm. Still wearing pants."

With her own release fading, she could feel Jay across their bond. He was aroused, still, but a smug satisfaction overwhelmed everything else, blunting the feral edge of dominance that had been riding him.

Jay was a man damn well pleased with himself, and she couldn't blame him. Her legs felt rubbery as she wrapped them around his hips and drew closer. "We should get you out of them. And get you into me."

"Dirty." He picked her up, stepped back and dropped to the bed with her in his lap. "Maybe just get them open?"

She wiggled back and fumbled with his fly, her fingers still clumsy. "You broke me. God damn it, Jay, you freaking broke me. I can't—" The button popped off and she yanked at his zipper. "Quit being pleased with yourself and help."

"Can't," he rasped. Helping involved waiting until she'd released his cock, then lifting her high and positioning her over him. "Quit being pleased with myself, I mean."

"So smug." Eden sank her fingers into his hair and jerked his head back. He might have satisfied the demands of possessiveness, but she'd barely gotten started. She licked the strong column of his throat with a growl. "I hope you won't be disappointed if I don't stay tamed for very long."

He trembled under her, every muscle tense and taut. "You never could be, honey."

"No." She relaxed her body enough to sink down. Not all the way, not even most of the way, just until the head of his cock pushed into her, then locked her knees. "How badly do you want to be inside me?"

"I can wait," he ground out between clenched teeth. "Are you going to make me?"

"Yes." So many ways to tease him. She rubbed her breasts against his chest. Scraped her teeth along his jaw in teasing bites only to follow with her tongue. "Wait. You have to wait."

But he didn't wait. He *moved*, and suddenly she found herself bent over the edge of the bed with Jay behind her, over her, his chest pressed to her back. "Wait?"

He wanted her. Needed her. Loved her. Passion and hunger throbbed between them, and she didn't need a magical bond to feel it. Restraint tensed his muscles, need set his heart to hammering against her back. She rocked back against him and gasped when his cock slicked through her folds and rubbed over her clit.

"Wait," she whispered, curling her fingers in the blankets. Her arms shook. "Wait until you can't stand it. Wait until you'll die if you don't take me."

His hands tightened on her hips, stilling her even as he took up her rocking motion. "You don't even know when that happened, do you?"

She'd needed him from the first shivering terror of being infected, but she'd wanted him for longer. "When I became a wolf?"

"Not even close." He licked a path up her spine. "I watched you before. I needed you."

A thousand casual interactions came back to her. Years of small talk and polite greetings, of passing each other in the street or crossing paths at the diner, but the wolf saw something else in her human memories. Self-denial in his eyes and protectiveness in his stance, an alpha alone and lonely and wanting what he couldn't have.

Maybe some part of her had always known. Maybe it had been fate all along. She was meant to be here, under him, alive because they fit together, body and soul.

"I didn't see," she whispered, twisting her head to meet his glazed, drowning dark eyes. "I wasn't ready."

He slid inside her with a sharp, indrawn breath. "And now?"

As if he had to ask. They fit together, all right, in the rawest, basest way imaginable. He pressed deep and she moaned at the perfect stretch, just enough to bring every nerve singing to life without pushing over the line into too much. She was meant to be like this, joined, one being shuddering together.

She dropped her head forward, baring the back of her neck as her hair swung around her face. "Show me what you've always wanted."

His mouth traveled higher, between her shoulder blades and finally to the nape of her neck. "It'll take years, Eden." He angled his hips back as he spoke, then drove deep with a groan.

Her body forgot that it had already been sated. Her knees buckled, spilling her onto the mattress, and then he was doing it again, gripping her hips and pulling her into the perfect position to shatter her sanity, and she didn't have the experience or the self-control to turn the tables on him. She couldn't reach him to stroke him to insanity or uncover the secrets of what touches made him wild.

But she could do something far more devastating. Pressing her cheek to the mattress, she melted for him, gave him one precious moment of submission along with the human equivalent. "I love you. You're mine."

Jay took both, closing his teeth on the vulnerable curve of her neck before whispering, "Love you too." The words rode a wave of emotion, love crashing over her tangled with lust and a dark, hungry satisfaction at her willing submission.

So much power in such tiny gestures. She wiggled, working her hands behind her until they nestled at the small of her back, trapped between their bodies, and the thrill it gave him turned helplessness into power. "Love me harder."

He hissed in a breath and reached between them to lock one hand around her wrists. "Yes, ma'am." Then he straightened, pulling her arms back to hold her suspended over the bed.

He'd used the Guide bond to master her body. She used it to claim his soul, following instinct to the deepest part of his heart, the not-so-human parts of him that craved the partnership of a strong mate and the submission of a strong lover.

She trusted him, and loved him, and she owned him when his control snapped and he took her.

Strong thrusts brought him into her again and again, each advance stripping another layer of humanity away. She groaned every time he slammed home, rasping encouragement in short, choppy pleas, crude words she couldn't remember knowing and couldn't believe she was saying.

"Eden." He ground out her name, the tension along their bond stretched taut like a bowstring. His free hand tangled in her hair, and he pulled her head back. "Now."

He wanted her to come. He needed it, the need so vast it swallowed her whole. All of his concentration was focused on her pleasure, on driving it to ridiculous heights with hard, carefully placed strokes, and knowing he'd do anything to earn her release tripped her over the edge.

The fall was beautiful. Heat cascading through her and she cried out, past dignity or reason as she rode her orgasm and he rode her.

Moments later, his pace sped. He rasped her name again and punctuated the whisper with one final, hard thrust. They fell through the bottom together, tumbling end over end in one another's release and crashing back to earth as one.

Eden didn't speak at first. She panted against the quilt as Jay eased her onto the bed and curled up behind her, his chest heaving as well.

As her heart rate slowed, a smile curved her lips. "You kinky bastard. You get off on that so hard."

He growled through a laugh and propped his head on her shoulder. "On what? On you?"

"On being the big bad alpha wolf." Feeling just as smug as he was, Eden caught his hand and twined their fingers together. "It's hot, how crazy it makes you."

"It wouldn't make me crazy if you didn't love it too. See the connection?"

"Works out pretty well, I suppose." She traced her fingertip over his hand in a loopy, mindless pattern. "We're a matched pair. A mated pair."

"An alpha pair." His fingers tightened around hers. "I don't think they can be honest with me about how they're doing yet, any of them."

"It'll take time, but they'll come around. And..." She smiled a little. "Lorelei. She doesn't trust me completely yet, but I like her, and she likes me. She'll help me take care of them, and Colin will help you protect them. We have backup."

"Betas," he murmured.

"Betas." She had to get at Shane's computer full of lore sooner rather than later. There was so much to learn about werewolves and pack, about the sanctuary they were going to build and the history of what she had become.

Tomorrow would be soon enough. Tonight she wanted to cuddle with her mate and enjoy the moment's peace. "Would it be rude or complimentary if I took a nap?"

Jay's laugh shook through her. "Passing out would be a compliment. A nap just sounds like a damn good idea."

"Next time," she mumbled, but it might have been a lie. Drained by the excitement of the past week and wrapped in the strength of his love and the warmth of his body, she tumbled toward oblivion.

Passing out was going to make Jay impossibly smug, but she didn't really care. He deserved it.

A three-hour nap through the evening was almost unforgivable, but Jay decided to let it slide—just this once. He emerged from the bedroom, bent on raiding the fridge for leftovers, but Mae and Stella were sitting at the kitchen table, talking quietly over mugs of hot cocoa.

Jay hastily finished buttoning his shirt. "Ladies."

Mae took in his disheveled appearance in her usual silence, but a small smile tugged at her lips as she rose to her feet. "I saved dinner for you and Eden."

He waved her back to her seat. "I don't think she'll be up before morning. She's exhausted."

"Bet she is, tiger." Stella raised an eyebrow at him over her mug.

"Not like that," he grumbled, pouring himself some cocoa from the pan on the stove. "What're you two up to?"

"Nothing." Stella flashed a look at Mae. "Talking about the farm, that's all."

"What about it?"

Mae wet her lips nervously. "The magic. We were talking about Stella's spells. She's cast a lot of them, along with some pretty impressive wards, but she's not tired like she should be."

Then she was the only one. He turned his attention to Stella. "How odd is that?"

"Mmm, hard to say." She shrugged. "Some places have power. It's in the earth, the air. The ether, I guess. Maybe this farm is one of them."

It explained plenty, from Eden's transformation before the pull of the full moon straight on back to the mysterious circumstances of Zack's conception. "Find out what it means, okay? For sure."

She inclined her head. "You got it."

Mae fiddled with her mug of cocoa, twisting it back and forth before giving Stella a significant look.

The witch responded instantly. "Yeah, well. I'm beat in a completely mundane, non-magical way, so I'm going to pack it in. Good night."

Jay watched as she set her mug in the sink and hurried out the door. Then he pulled out the chair opposite Mae's and sat. "What is it?"

Mae's gaze locked somewhere around his chin. "It's kind of silly."

He had to smile. "No, Mae. Whatever it is, it's not silly if it's important to you."

"It's just..." She swallowed hard, and her hand inched across the table, stopping just shy of his. "You're my alpha, and I've never really talked to you. But it matters to me, maybe more than it does to the rest of them. I need pack. My wolf's...weak."

Not weak, though how could she know that if she could barely touch the beast inside? "Are you having any control problems?"

She shook her head, sending pink hair flying. "She really only comes out at the full moon, or if another wolf..." Her jaw clenched, and fear and shame soured the space between them. "But that's not the same as control. I never really learned because I had a Guide, but she was one of the first wolves Christian killed."

Damn it. Jay covered her hand with his, moving slowly. "Then we'll need to find you another one."

"I know." Her voice faded to a small, scared whisper, but she clung to his hand as if it were the only solid thing in the world. "That's why I didn't tell you before... I don't know if I'm ready."

"You have time. If you were starting to shift without trying, anything dangerous like that, it'd have to be now. But you have time, Mae. Time to choose."

Her fingers clenched tight. "Thank you."

Don't. His first instinct, to deny her thanks. Deflect the gratitude that wafted around every single member of the pack like a tangible wave of sadness mixed with relief. "You're welcome."

He knew he'd made the right choice when her tension eased. She slipped her hand free of his and rose, only to circle the table and wrap one arm around his shoulders in a shy, tentative hug. "If Eden does wake up, her food's on the second shelf in the fridge. Yours is too."

"Thanks. I think I'm just going to lock up and head back to bed."

Mae smiled—a real smile—and swept up her cocoa. "Good night, Jay. Sleep well."

When the house was quiet, a stillness fell. More than the quiet, it seemed to seep from every wall, heavy somehow with echoes. Shadows you could just barely catch out of the corner of your eye, the kind that vanished when you turned to look.

Ghosts. That's what Eden had called them. Memories, Jay had said, and he still believed that. What had the old walls seen? What secrets did they carry?

He checked the front door before returning to the kitchen to flip the deadbolt on the back door. Before he could, a glimmer out by the barn caught his eye. White or beige, certainly not the shadows he was used to seeing in the darkness.

Jay pushed through the door. A breeze stirred his hair as well as a set of wind chimes on the back porch—Mae's doing, perhaps, or Lorelei's. They tinkled, underscored by a soft murmur.

The wind through the trees. Except the longer he listened, the more it sounded like a voice, words too low to make out.

He strode out toward the barn, the grass cool under his bare feet. His glimpse of the figure under the moonlight had been brief, but his mind already supplied details—human, feminine, dark hair.

The whispering stopped.

"Kaley, is that you?" He rounded the back of the barn, but nothing greeted him except trees and that damnable breeze.

Alpha.

The word crawled up his spine, sick and terrifying. It came from nowhere, and it came from right beside him. He whirled, his gaze snagging on a soft glow through the trees.

A woman stared at him, familiar somehow. Unsmiling. He watched, dumbstruck, as she shook her head, mouthed words and vanished.

Alpha. The word echoed again, sending another shiver up Jay's back, especially when the whisper continued. *Help him.*

No throb of magic, not a single sense on alert. Jay stood behind the barn, his heart pounding, and fought the urge to run like a damn boy. When he did move, he kept his pace measured, even, and walked back to the house.

The lock clicked behind him, and absent steps carried him into the den, where he'd stowed Eden's box of pictures, the ones she'd brought home the night before. His hands trembled as he pawed through them, and a stray shard of glass sliced his thumb.

"Fuck." He sucked away the blood and lifted the photo he'd been looking for, a sad shot on the front porch of the farmhouse. Zack's parents sat in rocking chairs, while he stood between them. His hands clenched so tightly around the straight chair backs that his knuckles stood out, stark and white, but that wasn't what held Jay's attention riveted.

Kathy Green, beautiful but melancholy. The woman in the photo.

The woman he'd seen outside.

Help him. Help them all.

About the Author

How do you make a Moira Rogers? Take a former forensic science and nursing student obsessed with paranormal romance and add a computer programmer with a passion for gritty urban fantasy.

To learn more about this romance-writing, crime-fighting duo, visit their webpage at www.moirarogers.com, or drop them an email at moira@moirarogers.com. (Disclaimer: crime-fighting abilities may appear only in the aforementioned fevered imaginations.)

It's all about the story...

Romance

HORROR

www.samhainpublishing.com

CPSIA information can be obtained at www.ICGtesting.com
Printed in the USA
LVOW12s2358070214

372912LV00004B/481/P